SHOESTRINGS—
NO TIME FOR DINOSAURS

SHOESTRINGS—
NO TIME FOR DINOSAURS

John Benjamin Sciarra

Wild Animal Publishing Company

Connecticut

Shoestring — No Time For Dinosaurs

All Rights Reserved © 2005 by John Benjamin Sciarra

Wild Animal Publishing Company

For more information please contact:
Wild Animal Publishing Company
3 Golf Ct.
Groton, CT 06340

Visit: www.johnbenjaminsciarra.com
Cover illustration by Keith M. Cowley

ISBN: 0-9769555-0-4

Library of Congress Control Number: 2005904102

Printed in the United States of America

This book is dedicated to my children, Lelah, Jamin and Anjuli and my grandchildren, Aaron and Noah.

ACKNOWLEDGEMENTS

I would like to thank Beth Bruno for doing an excellent job editing and Tabitha Jones for some great suggestions in the development of the story. I would also like to thank Maryanne Denobriga for reading my story to fourth and fifth grade classes and giving me excellent feedback, as well as the students at the Claude Chester Elementary School in Groton, Ct., for their comments and enthusiasm.

Thanks to Keith Cowley for not only the great illustration on the cover, but also excellent input for the dinosaurs as my resident paleontologist. Thanks, too, to Dan Uitti for his skills in formatting and other advice.

PART I

THE TIME CAPSULE

CHAPTER ONE

Kyle, Teresa and Sonja sat quietly in the laboratory lounge. Kyle, feeling fidgety, plopped his legs across the coffee table, accidentally spilling a can of Coke.

"Will you be careful!" said Teresa. She turned to Sonja and added, "You should be glad you don't have a brother."

"I'm bored. When's Dad coming back?"

Teresa and Sonja grabbed a handful of tissue and sopped up the soda.

"He said he'd only be a few minutes."

"That was a half hour ago," said Kyle with a sigh. "Let's go find him."

"My dad said we should wait here," said Sonja.

Kyle got up and went to the door. "There's no one in the lab. Where did they go?"

"Maybe upstairs," said Teresa. "Sonja's right. We should just wait."

A younger sister telling her older brother what to do was just asking for trouble. Kyle pushed the door open and went out.

"Kyle!" yelled Teresa. She rolled her eyes and ran after him with Sonja following close behind. Kyle had already entered the lab. Teresa tried the door, but it was locked.

"How did he get in?" asked Sonja.

"You have to know Kyle."

Teresa banged on the door but Kyle just made a face at her. She banged harder until finally Kyle let them in.

"Okay, how did you know the security code?"

"Dad pushed the buttons when he and Dr. Bashan went in. I saw which ones he pushed."

Teresa shook her head and rolled her eyes. "Be careful around my brother, Sonja. He'll get you into trouble pretty fast."

"I don't see our dads," said Kyle. "Let's look in the other lab."

"But there's a 'No Admittance' sign on the door," said Sonja. "You can read, can't you?"

Kyle ignored the younger girls. He was 14 and both of them were 12. They were like little babies to him. He pushed on the door, but it was locked.

The girls giggled. "Ha, ha. You can't get in that one. There's a scanner on it that checks your finger prints."

The two girls walked around the lab leaving Kyle to ponder his problem.

"Isn't there an elevator here?" asked Sonja.

"Yeah, I think there is."

Teresa and Sonja found the elevator at the end of a long corridor. Sonja pressed the call button. A keypad on the side lit up. It said; "Enter code now."

"Great," said Teresa. "Looks like a dead end. Let's grab Kyle and get out of here before he gets us in trouble."

The girls looked around in awe at all of the computers and tubes filled with thick green liquid that seemed to glow. Small, spiraled hoses ran the length of the large laboratory. Their curiosity sidetracked them. As they looked in wonder at all the equipment and experiments, they just stood there gawking.

***

Kyle remembered something he saw on TV once, a show where crime scene investigators lifted fingerprints from a latex glove. He wondered if his father or someone else used gloves in their work. *It wouldn't hurt to look*, he thought. Kyle hoped the cleaning people hadn't emptied the garbage yet.

He looked around the lab. There was nothing in the first can but a bag. It was the same with the second. In the third, however, there was a single glove at the bottom stuck in the fold of the bag.

Kyle took the glove out and carefully turned it inside out. He then pulled the glove on his own hand being careful not to touch the tips. It slipped on easily.

Kyle put his gloved hand against the reader and pressed the access button. The reader flashed green and read, "Authorized." Kyle turned the handle and went in.

***

Teresa and Sonja continued looking around the lab, but there was no sign of Kyle.

"Your brother must be very smart," said Sonja.

"That's not what Dad says. He does terrible in school. My dad grounded him for a month when he brought home four 'F's' and a 'D' on his report card."

Sonja was surprised. "How could he figure out how to get into the lab like that?"

Teresa was about to answer when all of the computers suddenly came on at once. The liquid in the tubes began to move and glowed bright green.

"What's happening?" asked Sonja.

Teresa looked shocked. "It must be Kyle!"

CHAPTER TWO

They ran to the locked door and began pounding on it. "Kyle, are you in there?" they shouted. A sign blinked above the lab that read: "Activation in Progress."

"Oh my god," said Teresa. "What has he done?"

There was a loud clicking sound and the girls backed away from the door. It slowly swung open. The door was thick like a bank vault door, at least a foot thick.

Kyle's head appeared around the corner. His eyes were wide with excitement.

"You guys have to see this!"

"Kyle, you shouldn't be in there. Get out before Dad finds out."

"Okay, okay, but you have to see this first!" Kyle responded as he pulled Sonja into the lab. "Come on, Teresa."

Concerned about being left alone, Teresa jumped through the door as it started to close. The girls' mouths dropped open when they saw a dome-topped cylinder encased in glowing green fluid.

"Oh my god!" exclaimed Teresa. "What is it?"

"I don't know," said Kyle.

"How did you turn it on?" asked Sonja as she touched the liquid. She noticed it wasn't actually enclosed in anything. It was just...there. A ripple shimmered through the liquid and it moved counter-clockwise. Sonja pulled her hand back frightened.

"Turn what on?" asked Kyle.

"All the computers. They came on all at once and the fluid started to move through the tubes."

"I didn't touch anything," he said as he put his hands on the gel surrounding the fluid. "Feel it. It's...cool to the touch. Like...cold Jell-O. Maybe you should taste it, Teresa. Maybe it's a giant lime Jell-O mold."

Teresa didn't respond. She and Sonja were too busy feeling the gel. They were fascinated how it appeared to respond to their touch and shimmered and moved.

As Kyle was exploring the gel he noticed that the air smelled familiar. He thought it smelled like the air after a thunderstorm. As he continued to explore with his hands, he suddenly felt the gel part. It actually opened up to let his hand through.

Teresa and Sonja watched in horror as Kyle disappeared into the cylinder.

"Kyle!" screamed Teresa. "Kyle!"

Kyle emerged two seconds later.

"Now that was weird! If you think it's strange out here, you should take a look from the inside. There's some kind of camera setup. It's really something. Come on. Take a look."

Kyle disappeared back into the capsule. The girls could just barely make out a shadowy figure inside waving at them.

Sonja pushed her hand into the fluid to test it and found herself inside with Kyle. He was inspecting a

7

camera seated on a tripod in the middle. The capsule wasn't very large, maybe four feet in diameter.

"What is this?" asked Sonja.

"That's what I'm trying to figure out. It looks like our dads are trying to videotape something, but I have no clue what they're doing."

Teresa popped through the opening. "I'm not staying outside by myself. It's getting noisy out there."

Kyle suddenly looked concerned. "What do you mean, noisy?"

"It sounded like...music, but not like a song or anything."

"What did it sound like?"

"Like a hundred violins playing all at once. It was kind of pretty, but getting louder."

Kyle looked deep in thought for a moment. Then it dawned on him what it might be. "Harmonics."

"What?" asked Sonja

"We have to get out of here...now!"

Kyle squeezed past Teresa and went to put his hand through the fluid door, but it didn't part like before. Now it felt solid.

"Uh oh."

A look of panic flashed across both the girls' faces as the wall began to move. Slowly at first. Then it began to pick up speed. They could hear the music now. It was like the sound of a hundred violins in perfect harmony.

***

"Okay, Paul, ready for launch. Is the camera set to auto?"

"Yes, David. I set it myself. Launch sequence initiated. Harmonics set to 50%."

"Once we launch, we better get back and check on the children. If I know my son, he won't sit still for long. Thanks for letting me know the capsule returned. It was gone, what...twenty days, right?"

"Correct, Dr. David. You really think the image is a dinosaur?"

"Either that, or a zoo with very strange animals. It was hard to tell through the gel. Something was there, that's for sure. There's no way to tell how far back it went. It could be anytime. Any time, but not any place. The capsule can't move. It should be right where it is now, but it emerged somewhere in time."

"Essentially correct. I guess we'll never know until we send a human. But we don't know...we just don't know if they'll survive."

"Let's go check on the kids. The capsule should be gone by now. Shut the sequence down."

"Sequence off. Okay, let's go."

CHAPTER THREE

Three frightened children watched as the fluid began to spin faster and faster. The music rose in volume and pitch. Kyle yelled above the noise, "Cover your ears and close your eyes!"

The girls did as the older and wiser Kyle suggested. No matter how hard they squeezed their ears though, the sound got through.

It kept climbing and climbing until they didn't think they could take it any longer. The walls were spinning faster and faster. The green gel shimmered and evaporated into what appeared to be water. It turned light blue and then all of the colors of the rainbow. The colors pulsated up and down. Then everything stopped.

Kyle opened his eyes. The walls were solid again and semi-transparent green. A strange light flashed outside and he thought he heard the distant sound of thunder. The girls were still standing there with their eyes squeezed tight and their fingers stuck in their ears. Kyle tapped Teresa on the shoulder and she slowly took her hands away and opened her eyes. Her teeth were clacking and she was shaking. She reached over and tapped Sonja's shoulder.

"Are we still alive?" asked Sonja.

Teresa asked, "Where are we?"

"More like, when," answered Kyle far too calmly.

"When?" asked Teresa.

"I think we just went back in time."

A noise inside the capsule caused them all to jump. Then the camera came on and began to pivot slowly. Teresa jumped in front of it.

"Dad? Help! We're here! Can you see us?" she yelled into the camera.

Kyle chided, "Why do you always have to ham it up whenever there's a camera around?"

"Stop fooling around, Kyle. We're stuck in here and all you can do is make fun of me."

"Sorry," he said as he turned to Sonja. "It's an addiction, you know. I've been to counseling, but I just can't seem to give it up."

Sonja couldn't help but giggle.

"Will you two get serious? Maybe our dads can see us. Dad, help!" Teresa had turned back toward the camera. "We're in here with Kyle. It's his fault. You should ground him..."

"For what? A million years? We could be hundreds—even thousands of years in the future...or the past."

"Don't say that, Kyle. Stop all this nonsense about time traveling. You're just trying to scare me. There's no such thing and you know it."

Kyle looked at Sonja. "What kind of scientist is your father?"

"He's a quantum physics theorist. I'm not sure what that means, though."

"I read some books on that. When I heard the sound of the violins and looked at all the fluid starting to move, I thought we might be in some kind of a time machine."

Teresa asked, "What does the music have to do with time machines? That's so stupid!"

"Not really, dummy. Scientists think that inside every little particle in the universe there's a little thread of electricity. These...strings...at least I think that's what they're called, are supposed to vibrate like music. Everyone knows that."

"Not everyone," said Sonja. She was clearly becoming infatuated with Kyle's knowledge. "I don't think very many adults know what string theory is."

"You mean you know what my dumb brother is talking about?"

"I heard my father talk about it to my mother. She is a physicist, too. But she doesn't agree with my dad. They have arguments all the time. My mom thinks Einstein's theory is correct and my dad keeps trying to convince her that you need both theories. I don't understand much about it. But Kyle may be right."

"What? We've gone back in time? Are you serious?" Teresa started yelling into the camera again. "Dad, help! We're stuck in here! Get us out!"

"Shhhh," whispered Kyle. "Listen."

In the background they could hear a heavy thumping and feel it through the bottom of the capsule.

"Is that...thunder?" asked Teresa.

"That's not thunder," said Kyle with a look of fear for the first time that day.

***

Dr. Donavan and Dr. Bashan ran around the lab frantically trying to find the children. When they had gone to the lounge, there was no sign of them. They searched the halls and ran to the cars. They ran back into the building and looked all over the lab. Now they were both standing in front of the empty space where the capsule had been. A shimmering shadow remained in the space, a consequence of the time distortion left by the capsule. It was what allowed it to return and was completely random when it happened. They could send it, but they couldn't bring it back.

"They could not have gone in the capsule. It is impossible!"

Dr. Donavan, however, knew his son all too well. He had gotten in trouble getting into places he shouldn't have. Despite Kyle's grades, Dr. Donavan knew his son had great potential. He just had no idea how to channel all that energy and curiosity. He looked around the floor and found a glove.

"Oh my god, they *are* in the capsule!"

"What? How could that be? That's impossible." Despite his protestations, Dr. Bashan was white as a ghost.

"This glove. It's inside out."

"So?"

"I'm guessing Kyle used it to gain access to the capsule. How on earth he got the girls to follow..." As he looked down near the distortion, he too looked pale. There on the floor was half a shoestring. He recognized it as Teresa's. It was bright pink. The odd thing about it was that only half of the string was visible, while the other half disappeared into the distortion field. Dr.

Donovan reached down and tried to pull on it, but it wouldn't budge. It was almost as if it wasn't there. He stood back up and looked over at Dr. Bashan. "How long was the capsule gone the last time?"

"Twenty days. What are we going to do?"

"Let's not panic."

"Not panic? My wife is going to panic. That means I must panic. We must find a way to get them back."

"How? We have no control over it. When the harmonics slow down enough, the capsule will slip back. We haven't a clue how long that's going to take. We don't even know where it is."

"Let's go back and see the tape again. Maybe it will give us more ideas about what it is we saw."

CHAPTER FOUR

Kyle squinted through the green gel to get a better look. The thumping sound was so close it caused the capsule to literally jump. Teresa continued her monologue with the camera hoping that somehow her dad might be able to see her. She couldn't have known it at the time, but it would help.

The thumping stopped. Whatever was out there was standing next to the capsule. All Kyle could see was an immense shadowy blob that appeared to be hovering over the capsule. All became very quiet. Even Teresa stopped talking and listened; her eyes were wide open with fear. Sonja moved next to Kyle. He stepped away.

A rumble of thunder trembled through the ground and the gel shimmered. Then a flash of lightning illuminated the shadow. Kyle gulped as he got a clear look at what was outside. The girls saw the look in Kyle's eyes and that was enough to scare them. They screamed.

***

Dr. Donavan sat at the computer and watched as the numbers scrolled across the screen. He was trying desperately to pinpoint how similar the harmonics were to the previous trip. He hoped that by doing so he'd be able to calculate when the capsule would come back in time

Time, he thought. We don't even know what it is and here we are messing around with it. Dr. Donavan wasn't even sure if they had gone anywhere. Maybe they had simply phased out of existence and back in — kind of like Star Trek's transporter. The camera had come back in one piece, but compared to a human, a camera was a fairly simple thing.

The numbers stopped scrolling and a figure came up on the screen. It had to be wrong.

***

Dr. Bashan was trying to improve the picture on the film from the camera. There was something there and it appeared to be moving. He thought it was some kind of animal, but nothing came to mind. He rewound the tape and tried adjusting the picture again. It looked to him like the head of an animal. It was only there for a second. He rewound more slowly until the picture froze on the image. Then he adjusted the contrast a little at a time.

Dr. Donavan peeked over his shoulder and the film shuddered.

"Oops. Sorry. I just wanted to see if you were making any progress."

"I have an image I'm trying to bring into focus. How are you doing with the calculations?"

"Not very well. I'm getting weird numbers. It doesn't make any sense."

"Why? When do the numbers indicate the capsule will return?"

Suddenly the picture focused. They stared at it in disbelief.

Dr. Donavan gulped. "Fifty or sixty years from now."

CHAPTER FIVE

Whatever was outside the capsule ran away when the girls screamed. They sat down completely exhausted and leaned against the cool surface of the gel. Kyle hadn't realized it before, but the gel was the only thing between them and whatever was outside. In the darkness of night he couldn't be sure where the door opening was located, or even if he wanted to know. All of them fell asleep.

When they awoke, they had no idea how much time had passed. Kyle chuckled despite himself. Time, he thought, echoing the words of his father without realizing it. What is it, anyway?

It was quiet outside. The whirring of the camera had stopped: it had run out of film. Kyle moved it aside to give them more room.

"How long have we been asleep?" asked Sonja stretching as she stood up. She was a pretty Eastern Indian girl with long black hair and dark eyebrows. There was no hint of an accent like her father's. She had been born in the United States in New York. Neither Kyle nor Teresa had ever met her before today. Her parents didn't even let her attend school. Instead, she was home-schooled.

In contrast, Kyle and Teresa were fair-skinned Irish descendants with a little Spanish from their mother's side. Teresa's hair was auburn with a hint of reddish scarlet. She had a face full of freckles. Kyle had dirty blond hair that seemed to propel itself every which way. At fourteen, he had finally broken free of his mother's grease gun and let his hair do whatever it wanted. His hair was a little like his personality — free and wild.

Kyle hated school. It was sooooo boring, he thought. Teachers made him do the same simple equations over and over again. He'd tell them he understood, but they wouldn't believe him. So he stopped trying to convince them. They were all pretty stupid anyway. He much preferred to read on his own.

Teresa was reluctant to get up. She put her hand in front of her mouth and breathed while trying to sniff at the same time.

"What are you doing? There's nobody here going to care what your breath smells like, dragon girl."

"How do you know?"

"That...thing outside the capsule last night? I think it was a dinosaur of some kind."

Teresa jumped up and tried to feel her way around the gel. She was starting to panic. Kyle was instantly sorry he had said that. He knew this was no time to fool around.

"Calm down, Teresa. You scared..."

Before Kyle could finish his sentence, Teresa fell through the opening and was on the other side. Sonja put her hands to her mouth in shock. "Oh no!"

Kyle felt around and found the opening and followed Teresa. Sonja didn't want to be left alone and followed as well. When Sonja came through she bumped into Kyle who was standing motionless. Even Teresa was standing perfectly still, her eyes fixed on the scene in the valley below. A thick cloud rose from the ground giving the impression they were standing on a high mountain. Lush vegetation jutted above the thick fog and filled the horizon. The trees and plants were bizarre looking. It was as if they had been transported to an alien planet. What had caught their attention, however, wasn't the scenery itself. Down in the valley was a herd of large dinosaurs eating leaves off of a cluster of tall trees that resembled tropical palm trees.

Teresa broke the silence. "Where are we?"

"I told you I saw a dinosaur. It must have been one of those things. They look pretty harmless—like a bunch of giant cows."

Sonja crinkled her nose. "What is that smell? It's— horrible!"

Kyle looked next to the capsule and pointed toward an enormous pile of brown. It was covered with gigantic, fly-like insects buzzing all around.

"I think our visitor left us a present."

"Oh, gross!" exclaimed Teresa. "Let's get out of here."

"Believe me, I'd like nothing better than to get out of here. I looked all over the capsule and there are no controls anywhere. It has to be controlled from the lab somehow. Our dads will discover us missing and bring the capsule back." Kyle thought for a minute. "And then he'll ground me for a hundred years. Maybe we should stay here."

Sonja said, "Then we should stay in the capsule. If it leaves…" her eyes got wide.

Something screeched overhead and a dark shadow crossed over them.

"What the heck was that?" asked Kyle. "Let's get back in the capsule. Right now. Sonja's right. It's the only way back."

Teresa started pushing on the gel at the spot she came out. It was solid. She looked down when something caught her eye. It was her shoestring. She tried to grab it but it wouldn't budge. It appeared to be frozen in the gel.

Kyle and Sonja joined her and started feeling around for the opening. Then they heard what sounded like a hundred violins and the gel began to move. The dinosaurs stopped eating and looked in the direction of the capsule. Kyle, Teresa and Sonja backed away in horror as the gel began moving faster and faster. They grabbed at their ears as the music reached a high pitch. There was a shimmer—and then the capsule was gone.

CHAPTER SIX

"It looks like the pictures I saw of the Loch Ness Monster," remarked Dr. Donavan.

"How far back did we send them?"

"We can't even be sure we sent them to the same period. Clearly we have sent them back in time. But how far? If they…"

They were interrupted by the sound of violin-like harmonies. Immediately, they recognized its implications. The capsule was returning. Both men jumped up and ran to the vault-like door and waited for the green light to go in. Their stomachs felt like they were in their throats.

The music ended abruptly and Dr. Donavan placed his hand against the reader. The door made a loud clicking sound and then slowly opened. They both tried to squeeze through the door even before it was fully opened. There in the middle of the room was the glowing green capsule. The children were gone.

***

Kyle sat down in the middle of the strange field. Teresa and Sonja were crying.

"This is all your fault, Kyle!" Teresa wailed. "Now we'll never see Mom and Dad again!"

Kyle tried to defuse the situation with his usual inappropriate humor. "Look on the bright side. No more homework." It was halfhearted and the girls knew it. "We have to get out of here. Look. The dinosaurs are starting to move in our direction. Even if they are harmless, I don't want to get stepped on."

"But what if the capsule comes back for us?" asked Sonja. "Shouldn't we stay here?"

Two of the large beasts were already coming up the hill to investigate. It was all they needed to see to convince them Kyle was right. They ran for a small clump of trees and hid behind them and watched. Teresa was shivering.

"It's going to be okay. If Dad was smart enough to invent a time capsule, he'll find a way to come back and get us," said Kyle. They watched as a herd of about twelve dinosaurs sniffed at the ground where the capsule had been. They were about fifteen feet tall with long slender necks and pointed snouts. Their faces were docile and peaceful looking. Their thick bodies ended in long heavy tails they dragged behind them. Kyle figured they must weigh over ten tons.

Something came up behind Teresa and she screamed when it touched her leg. It was wet and sticky. The large dinosaurs stopped sniffing and looked over at the clump of trees.

"Are you trying to get us killed?" yelled Kyle. Then he saw something rush off in a blur and practically fly to the top of a nearby tree. "What was that?"

"I don't know. It...touched me. It was icky. Yech!"

Sonja looked over at Teresa's leg. "Where?" She was concerned. "Did it bite you?"

"I don't think so. It felt...like a wet towel with syrup on it." Teresa shivered.

Kyle looked back at the dinosaurs that had resumed their sniffing. Something about the capsule seemed to attract them to it. A rustling from the treetop told him their visitor was still there. He wondered if anything else would be coming to visit.

Sonja had picked a leaf and was wiping the spot on Sonja's leg with it.

"Do you think that's such a good idea? We don't know if that leaf is poisonous or not. We should observe the dinosaurs and see what they touch before we touch anything."

Sonja nodded. If she had to be lost in time, she was glad it was with Kyle. Then again, she thought, it was Kyle's fault they were there in the first place.

"It seems okay. It's not red or anything. Does it hurt?"

"No. It seems okay."

Kyle observed, "Our visitor is back. He's behind that tree over there."

The two girls watched and hugged each other, then slowly moved behind Kyle. Kyle was curious and cautiously walked over to the tree and bent down to see what was there. Two blinking eyes peered out at him from behind the tree. The eyes were large, and though the animal appeared slightly frightened, its curiosity was overwhelming. No doubt it had never seen a creature like Kyle before. Humans wouldn't arrive on the earth for another 64 million years or so.

Kyle reached out with his palm down as if it were a dog. He had no idea what else to do. He only hoped it wouldn't decide to take a bite.

The creature backed away a little and Kyle got a better look at it. It didn't look like any dinosaur he had ever seen in a book or whose bones were in a museum.

It appeared to be delicate—almost birdlike in its structure and movement. It had no wings, however. It wasn't much larger than the family's dog, a miniature pincher, and it appeared about as nervous.

Kyle kept his hand extended and tried not to make any sudden movements. He spoke to the girls behind him in a whisper. "Don't move or you'll scare it. I want to see if it will come to me."

The girls needed no coaxing. They weren't about to move unless something frightened them to action. They were still frozen in fear and shivering.

The creature stuck its neck out very slowly and then jerked back. It reached out again and took a sniff of Kyle's hand. Kyle stayed perfectly still. The girls were watching in wide-eyed horror.

"He's kinda cute," Kyle whispered. "Come on there, doof-a-saurus. I won't hurt you."

Then the creature opened its mouth and Kyle's blood froze. It had a mouthful of sharp teeth running from one end clear to the other. Small or not, Kyle knew this animal could do damage if it wanted. Rather than startle it, Kyle left his hand where it was and fought the urge to pull back out of fear. The animal sensed the change and backed away. Without warning, it opened its mouth and let out a screeching sound.

The girls screamed in response, but Kyle held his ground. He knew enough about animals to know that if he ran, it would chase him down. He treated it much as he would an angry dog. He stood up to his full height of 5' 7" and stared the animal down. The creature's response was to look down at the ground in submission. Apparently, thought Kyle, the pecking order is the same here as it will be in the future.

"What do you think we should do with him?" asked Kyle.

Sonja asked, "What is it?"

"I'm not really sure," said Kyle scratching his head. The creature watched with rapt interest at every movement Kyle made. "It reminds me of the *Velociraptor*, but without the hooked talons. See the front foot? Remember those things from the Jurassic Park movie?"

"The ones that chased the kids and ripped everybody to shreds?" exclaimed Teresa with fear in her eyes.

"Yeah. But this one's a baby…I think."

Sonja looked around. "Where's his mom and dad? I don't think we should be playing with him. What if they get mad? Really. We should go."

"Where? The capsule's gone. We can't leave the area in case it comes back, can we? We have to find somewhere to hold out for a while. Maybe we could build a lean-to."

"What about the creature? What if he follows us?"

"I'm open to suggestions, ladies." The creature was sniffing Kyle's leg and trying to taste the material. "Hey! Get outta there, you doof-a-saurus."

The creature cocked its head as if trying to understand what Kyle was saying. Then it made jerky head bobbing motions while squealing.

"Now look what you did, Kyle. You hurt its feelings," said Teresa as she moved over to the creature and kneeled down to the ground. It came right over to her and put its head in her lap. *Just like my dog*, she thought. Teresa stroked its head. "It feels...weird. It looks like feathers, but feels more like a crocodile's skin or something like that. I think it likes me!"

Kyle was astonished and just stood there with his mouth open. "I can't believe it!"

"What? That it likes me?"

"No. That it has such bad taste in people!"

Teresa ignored him. Sonja came over and leaned down to the creature as well and began to stroke its head. "It does feel like...like...leather. It isn't very pretty. None of these animals are very pretty. I thought they would all be so colorful. The ones in the books and the movies all look...beautiful!"

"Yeah," said Kyle. "I noticed that, too. Not even the plants are very colorful. I mean...everything's green, but its such a dark green. And the stink. It smells like...like...what does it smell like?"

"Like sulfur?" said Teresa.

"That's it," said Sonja. "It smells like sulfur. And did you notice how wet we are?"

"I'm soaked!" said Teresa. "I was so shocked, I didn't even notice. The air is so thick. It's like..."

"...fog!" finished Kyle. "The air is thick with water. I'll bet it doesn't even rain here. It's like a tropical rain forest!"

The large dinosaurs began leaving the hill to return to their fertile valley. All agreed that Kyle's idea of building a lean-to was a good one and they began gathering branches. The small raptor followed the girls, running first to one and then the other and watched them with wide eyes. They wanted to have the shelter built by evening. From there they would watch and wait for the sound of a hundred violins signaling their rescue.

CHAPTER SEVEN

Dr. Donavan and Dr. Bashan sat at the computer screen and ran the videotape. They were startled when Teresa suddenly popped up crying for help. Tears welled up in the doctors' eyes. They felt so helpless. All their science and math and technical ability couldn't bring the children back.

"We have to send the capsule back," said Dr. Donavan. "I don't know what else we can do. At least we know they were transported in one piece."

"Why can't we go back for them?" said Dr. Bashan excitedly.

"Hmm. That's a good idea. Let's set up one more test first—just in case. We can remount the video camera and set it the same way as before. Then we'll wait for the capsule to come back. If the kids are nearby, they might even jump back on! That way we'll know for sure."

"Wonderful idea. If we can get them back today, we won't have to tell their mothers."

"If they come back, the whole world is going to know. Set everything exactly the same as the last time. Then, let's send the capsule back.

***

Once they had made their lean-to out of leaves and branches, Kyle went back over to the place where the capsule had been. There were enormous piles of droppings from the large dinosaurs. He remembered that they were called *Apatosaurus*. They were thought to be the largest dinosaurs ever to walk the earth—and he had actually seen one. He hoped he would be able to return and tell people what it was really like. He had seen so many movies and read so many books about dinosaurs. To actually see a living creature, he thought. No one has ever seen anything like this! Unless, of course, they came back in time, too. But, if that were the case, wouldn't he have seen someone from the future? Unless…he didn't get back and they abandoned the idea all together! He told himself to stop thinking like that. It was scaring him.

He knew the girls were counting on him. He had to be the man. He had to be the leader. As he wandered around the area where the capsule had been, he was careful not to stand directly in its place. He wasn't sure what would happen if it landed on him, and he didn't want to find out.

In the grass he saw Teresa's shoestring. Odd, he thought. It's only half a shoestring. He reached down and tried to pick it up, but it was as if it wasn't there. Kyle stood back up and scratched his chin and tried to think about why the string was acting so peculiar. It meant something, but he wasn't sure what. He'd have to give it some thought. Besides, it was getting dark already; that was odd because he didn't think they had been up all that long.

It was then that he realized the sky was streaked with black clouds and he could hear the sound of distant thunder. Maybe it did rain. "Of course! A rain forest," he said out loud and ran back to the girls who were chasing the doof-a-saurus around the lean-to.

"Let's get inside and put branches over the front. I think it's going to rain," said Kyle. The raptor ran through his legs and into the lean-to and stood in the middle and bounced up and down.

"I think Priti wants us to come in after her," said Sonja.

"Pretty? You named this ugly thing Pretty?"

"Don't say that out loud," scolded Teresa. "Besides, that's P-r-i-t-i. And be careful. You'll hurt her feelings!"

"Whatever. How do you know it's a girl?"

"We don't. We just decided that's what we think it is and wanted to give it a name. If we call her Priti, she'll think she is."

"Oh come on. You don't believe it understands, do you?"

"Priti!" said Teresa. "Come!" The raptor ran back through Kyle's legs and over to her and sat with its strange-looking claws outstretched. It screeched and Teresa handed it a piece of what looked to be bark.

"See? She knows her name."

Kyle rolled his eyes. "Women."

"At least you admit it."

The thunder sounded closer and the sky glowed with orange and white flashes of lightning. Priti seemed nervous. Kyle thought that was strange since he figured the animal would be used to it if it were a common occurrence. If it were frightened, then maybe there was cause for concern.

He looked down where the Apatosaurus had been foraging and was surprised that they weren't there anymore.

"Did you guys see the big dinosaurs leave?" "No," said Sonja. "I didn't hear anything."

"Me neither," said Teresa. "Why? Does it matter?"

"Well, your little raptor there seems frightened of the storm."

"So? I'm frightened of it, too. What of it?"

"Wouldn't you think he…"

"She!" said Teresa leaning down and petting the animal.

"She…should be used to it if this happens a lot. It was thundering yesterday when we arrived in the capsule."

"Like I said, so?"

"This must not be something…normal. Maybe something's going on. We really don't know very much about this time period."

"What time period? You mean you know what time we went back to?"

"Not exactly. Millions of years, if there are large dinosaurs here. More than sixty million anyway."

"What makes you say that?"

Sonja answered. "Because the dinosaurs became extinct about sixty million years ago."

"Oh? How did they become extinct?"

Kyle replied, "From a comet that hit the earth near Mexico. At least that's what most scientists think."

Sonja asked with a little nervousness in her voice, "Do you think that's what is happening? I mean, this storm?"

"Nah. What are the chances of arriving right when the comet is going to hit? Heh, heh." Kyle said, but there was uncertainty in his answer. He wanted to believe that wasn't possible. He also wanted to believe that time travel was impossible, but here they were.

They all sat down in the back of the lean-to and Kyle replaced the branches over the entrance. The thunder grew louder and louder. Priti was shaking all over, just like the three children were.

CHAPTER EIGHT

The sound of a hundred violins filled the laboratory. It grew louder and louder, higher and higher. The doctors watched from outside the room through a window. The green gel began to move. Slowly at first. Then it increased in speed as it swirled like a miniature tornado.

As the violins reached their peak, the gel turned clear like water and then it pulsated with all of the colors of the rainbow. Then it was gone.

Dr. Bashan looked at his friend. "Well? Now what?"

"Now we wait."

Dr. Donavan went into the chamber area for no good reason except to stare into the shimmering void left by the capsule. He hoped they were right and it would return as quickly as it had the last time. They had set everything exactly the same as before. He saw no reason it wouldn't arrive back in time at the precise moment and place the children had gone. He expected them to get back on and return safely. As much as he wanted that to happen, he was anxious — more anxious than he had ever been in his life. To his knowledge, no one had ever gone back in time before. He wondered if he had changed the future with time travel. If so, why hadn't he been visited by travelers from the future? The whole idea gave him a headache and didn't make him feel any better. There was nothing they could do but wait.

***

The storm raged all that night and into the next day. It seemed there was no chance it would stop anytime soon. The girls were quiet and tried to sleep as much as possible. They were feeling nervous but getting a little used to the constant flashes of lightning and rumbles of thunder that came and went.

A break in the storm came some time later. The girls immediately fell asleep, but Kyle couldn't shut his eyes. It was nighttime and there were clouds still moving across the moon.

Seeing the moon made him feel good. It was something he recognized and it looked the same now as it would in the future with the exception of its color. It was blood red. *Probably the result of gases in the upper atmosphere that were different*, thought Kyle. Even though the storm was noisy, there was almost no rain. There was just the ever-present rolling fog soaking his shirt through to his skin.

As Kyle watched the clouds cross the path of the moon, all of the sudden the raptor jumped up and began sniffing the air. It moved back and forth with jerky head movements and appeared to be agitated — even frightened of something. Then, without warning, it bolted out of the lean-to and went running across the open field squealing like an injured pig.

Kyle became concerned. He knew animals could sense things before people. He wondered what it was that scared the creature so badly. Then he saw something moving just beyond the trees where the capsule had been. It was big and it wasn't an Apatosaurus. He recognized the shape from the movies. It was a T-Rex.

***

The weeks turned into months; the months to years. The heartbroken parents consoled each other. No one blamed the doctors. It had been an extremely unfortunate accident that led to the disappearance of their children. They had no choice but to get on with their lives. Still, the funeral was a difficult thing for everyone. No one wanted to accept that they were gone forever.

Dr. Donavan couldn't understand why the capsule hadn't returned. They had been so careful about sending it back to where the children had gone. He was upset for not going back in time himself.

He and Dr. Bashan had tried to build another capsule with contributions from the community, but few people believed it anyway. They just felt sorry for them. Most thought their children had simply been vaporized.

The Homeland Security agency banned their work altogether. They examined the videotape and concluded that the kids had been transported to another dimension and probably would be lost forever. No argument or scientific evidence prevented the agency from banning research into time travel. They felt it was an area of science too dangerous for humankind to deal with.

Before long, the families returned to their lives and moved on. Dr. Bashan went back to India with his wife and became a university professor. Dr. Donavan was a little more stubborn and kept his laboratory open for research in quantum physics. He let students use the facility to study the universe and the very tiny particles that made up everything.

He taught the students about the little strings of energy inside each and every one of the particles that make up the neutrons and electrons of every atom in the universe. He told them that one day they would be able to vibrate the strings and move about in the universe like never before. Most of the students thought he was simply a mad scientist, but they got to use his elaborate laboratory for their experiments for free—if they listened to him.

Doctor Donavan, however, had almost given up hope. Locked in the vault where the capsule had been was the distortion field. It still shimmered as it had done so many years ago on that fateful day—a day when three little children had gone inside and taken a trip into eternity. Before Dr. Donavan had sealed the lab, he tried one last time to remove the tiny pink shoestring sitting on the floor, half in and half out of the distortion field. As long as it was there, he thought, there was always hope his precious little children would return. That little piece of shoestring was his only link to sanity. It was a memorial to his beloved children—and a thread to the past.

CHAPTER NINE

Kyle tapped the girls on the shoulder and held up his hand. "There's something outside. Be very quiet."

Scared, Teresa asked in a whisper, "What is it?"

"Now don't freak out, but I think it's a T-Rex."

Both girls inhaled sharply. Sonja said, "A T-Rex? What are we going to do? Where's Priti?"

"Your creature double-feature ran off like the chicken hawk she—it is. It left us here on our own."

The ground shook from the approaching beast; it appeared to be sniffing the ground.

"We need to leave the lean-to. It's heading this way. I think it smells us."

"Maybe it's friendly like Priti," said Sonja somewhat hopefully.

"And if not? Do you want to see if it eats us first? I don't think I want to find out the hard way. Ya know, if it eats us, that's it. We don't get to change our minds. We can only be eaten once. So…"

"Okay!" said Teresa. "We get it. What should we do?"

"Okay, here's the plan. We lift up the back of the lean-to and crawl…"

"Crawl? Like…on the ground?" interrupted Teresa.

"Do you want to stay here?"

Teresa shook her head.

Kyle continued. "Okay. We crawl out the back. Very, very, quietly. We can't make any noise. Follow me down to the clump of big trees I saw earlier over by the place where we first saw your pet. Okay?"

"Then what?" Asked Sonja.

"Then we hide behind them."

"Oh. Good plan. I think we should stay here."

They heard the sound of distant thunder again. Streaks of orange flashed across the horizon.

"Hey, maybe it's afraid of the thunder? Like Priti," said Teresa.

"Well, let's just get away from here before it picks up our scent."

Kyle reached over to pull back the first branch when the lean-to was shaken with a loud, deep grumbling roar.

"Run," shouted Kyle as he threw back the branches and ran across the field to the trees. The girls didn't hesitate. They screamed and chased after Kyle. Lightning streaked from the sky and hit the ground just outside the lean-to. Kyle saw the T-Rex standing right over the lean-to. It looked up and roared at the sky with its tiny little front arms and enormous head and mouth full of long, sharp teeth. It seemed to Kyle it was more confused than angry as it sulked off down the hill toward the valley. In the process, however, it had stepped on their lean-to and flattened it like a pancake.

The storm came in quickly and was much more intense than before. The air was alive with electricity.

Bolts of lightning were hitting the ground everywhere they looked.

"We should get out from under this tree," observed Sonja. "It might be hit by lightning."

Teresa and Kyle both agreed, but it meant leaving the area where the capsule had been.

"I guess we can come back here when the storm passes," said Kyle. "I know this is going to sound like a crazy idea, but I think we should follow the T-Rex."

"You seem to have a lot of crazy ideas. Isn't that how we wound up here in the first place? Hey, where's my sneaker? I lost it when we ran out of the tent."

"I saw your shoestring," replied Kyle. "It's over by where the capsule was."

"And you didn't get it? Some brother!"

"I tried, but I couldn't."

"You just didn't want to. You're so mean to me."

"No, really. That wasn't it. You know I'd take credit for that if it were true. I mean I reached down for it, but only half of it was showing. The other half...disappeared into the area where the capsule had been. When I tried to pick it up and pull on it, my fingers went right through the strings. Like I said. It's like it wasn't there."

"You're not teasing me, are you?"

"Not this time. I know it must mean something, but I don't know what. Any ideas?"

"Well, I'd like to know where my sneaker is before we leave the area. I can't walk around here with one shoe on and one shoe off, can I?"

"Okay. Let's go over to the lean-to and see if we can find it."

The three children walked over to the flattened lean-to and looked through the brush. Sonja found the shoe. It was undamaged. Teresa put it on and Kyle grabbed a piece of root to tie it shut. They walked down to the valley hoping the lightening wouldn't hit down there — and they hoped the T-Rex had moved on.

They didn't see her, but Priti was following closely behind them.

CHAPTER TEN

They found a clump of bushes and crawled under them into a small clearing in the center after making sure there wasn't anything inside. A cluster of hanging branches with thick leaves protected it. No rain fell from the storm, but the air smelled somewhat cleaner now. The dampness was still heavy and they couldn't see a thing when they looked out through the brush.

A rustling sound caused them to jump back inside.

"What was that?" asked Sonja. "You think the T-Rex is back?"

"It doesn't sound big. But it could be anything."

"Like a Velociraptor?" asked Teresa with concern in her voice.

"Shhh," said Kyle.

A head suddenly popped through the brush and the girls screamed. Kyle jumped behind the girls. It was a second before they realized it was Priti and she was cooing at Teresa.

"Priti! Where have you been?" she asked as the creature stumbled through the brush and plopped down near her and Sonja. Priti hissed at Kyle who cautiously peeked out from behind his sister.

"She doesn't seem to like you. And you thought she had bad taste!"

"That...thing has a mouthful of razor sharp teeth. It must be a meat-eater. A carnivore. Like the T-Rex. It'll probably grow up to be fifteen feet tall and eat the two of you some day."

"Well, I hope we're not here long enough to find out!" exclaimed Sonja. "By the way, shouldn't we get back up to the top of the hill and wait for the capsule?"

"I guess so." Kyle seemed reluctant.

"What's the problem?" asked Teresa.

"I just don't want to run into anything. I'm sure there are a lot more dinosaurs out there that we haven't seen yet. Like the thing that screeched over head?"

"What do you think it was?"

"Maybe a *Pterosaur*? If they're anything like I read about, they make the T-Rex seem tame. I guess we should go. Just keep your heads low and listen carefully for any sounds."

"We'll have Priti to tell us if there's anything coming," remarked Teresa proudly.

"That's true. If we're in danger she'll run off like a chicken!"

Priti hissed at Kyle again, but then put her head back in Teresa's lap.

"Come on. Let's go," ordered Kyle.

They walked low to the ground while Priti darted about like a small dog jumping up and down begging to have someone play with her. It ran over to Kyle and grabbed his pant leg and pulled while making growling sounds.

"Hey, what's with this thing?"

"It just wants to play," said Sonja. "Maybe it's warming up to you after all. Maybe...it likes you!"

"Not a chance," said Teresa. "Who would like my brother? No one sane. Maybe a crazy person."

42

"I think he's very, very smart. Someday, he'll be a famous scientist," replied Sonja with a twinkle in her eye.

"Only if someday is sixty million years from now. What are we going to do if the capsule doesn't come back? We could be stuck here forever! There are no malls here! I don't even have a hairbrush. And where's the toilet paper? I need toilet paper! I miss my mom." Teresa was on the verge of tears.

Sonja put her arm around her and tried to console her. "I miss my mom, too. And I miss my *mataar paneer*. It's my favorite Indian food. In fact, I miss food! We haven't eaten anything. I just realized it!"

Kyle added, "You're right. We've been so busy trying to stay alive, we forgot to eat. What are we going to eat?"

Talking about food perked Teresa up a little and she quickly forgot about her sadness. "I saw some berries near where the lean-to was. Priti was eating them. Do you think that means they're safe?"

I guess there's only one way to find out. Teresa, you get to try them. You're our guinea pig."

"Not! I say you try them first."

"I'll try them," volunteered Sonja. "I don't mind. If Priti can eat them, I'm sure they won't be poisonous."

"Well, let's just get there first."

No sooner had Kyle said that, than they heard a screech from overhead and a large shadow passed over them.

***

The children sat down next to the berry tree and passed around the berries they had picked. They looked a little like giant raspberries but were the size of apples. Sonja thought they tasted more like strawberries, but Kyle insisted they were too sour to be strawberries.

Priti sat next to Kyle and nibbled on the leaves from the berry bush.

"Looks like Priti has a new friend," said Sonja.

"Yeah. I'm a little jealous. Why does she like you all the sudden?"

"I guess I'm the alpha male. She knows who's in charge."

"Oh brother! The alpha male. Head chicken in the pecking order maybe."

"Hey, I got us this far. Don't I get a little credit?"

"You mean like getting us stuck here in the first place?"

Before Teresa even finished her sentence, the ground began to shake violently. Kyle tried to stand, but fell back over and landed hard on the ground. Priti took off running across the ground falling and flopping all over the place and squealing loudly. They heard animals roaring and screeching from the valley below. The earth moved in waves as if the ground had suddenly turned into ocean. It lasted a few minutes and then stopped abruptly.

CHAPTER ELEVEN

"What was that?" asked Teresa.

"I think it was an earthquake."

"Is it over?" asked Sonja.

Kyle stood up again on somewhat shaky legs and looked around. "Probably not. Look over there. See? In the distance beyond the valley?" Kyle pointed toward the horizon. A cone shaped mountain was spewing out thick black smoke. Right at its top—its apex—they could see a glowing red and yellow fire spitting rocks out in all directions.

"Are we in danger staying here?" asked Sonja.

"I don't think so. At least not yet. I sure hope our dads send the capsule back soon. I don't like this place."

"I second that," said Teresa.

"Me too," added Sonja.

Priti came sulking back and nuzzled up against Teresa.

"There's no dinosaurs anywhere in the valley. Did you notice that? They're all gone," observed Teresa as she stroked Priti's head. "Something scared them even before the earthquake."

"That can't be a good sign. Animals always know when something bad is going to happen."

"That doesn't make me feel any better, Kyle. Maybe the volcano is going to explode and kill us all...like in Pompeii. Maybe we should leave, too."

"We can't leave. We have to stay near this spot. The capsule can't materialize in another location, unless they move it in the future."

"Well, maybe they'll do that."

"They wouldn't even know why that would be necessary, Teresa. I know this is scary. I'm scared, too. I just don't have any answers. I just know we have to stay here — even if it means we're risking our lives."

Sonja said without thinking, "That's so brave! We will stay here. I will be brave, too."

Teresa felt obligated to agree, although she didn't really feel very brave. Still, she knew Kyle was right. She hated that about him.

A burst of hot gases and smoke came pouring out of the volcano and the earth shook violently again. They all fell to the ground in a pile.

"I don't think I'm feeling very brave anymore," said Sonja. Now she too had tears in her eyes.

They all heard a loud whizzing sound coming from above. Kyle looked up half expecting to see a Pterosaur swooping down on him. Instead he saw a giant flaming ball arching across the sky in their direction.

He screamed, "Run! Get out of here, now!"

All of them, including Priti, ran as fast as they could across the hill and hid behind a group of trees. They knew it wouldn't help, but there was nowhere else to go — nowhere to hide.

It moved across the sky as if in slow motion leaving a trail of black smoke in its wake. Then it slammed into the valley below and burst into flames as it ignited the brush and trees around it. The ground shook again and knocked them off their feet.

"Oh my god!" said Teresa. "That landed right where we were staying! Oh my god, oh my god! What are we going to do?" Teresa was sitting on the ground with her legs curled up under her. Priti was nuzzled right up against her with her head under Teresa's legs trying to hide. They were both shivering.

Before Kyle could answer the sky became dark again quite suddenly. He looked up and saw an object moving across the sky very slowly. It glowed and had a long glowing white tail behind it. Unlike the rock they had just seen land in the valley, however, it appeared to be far out in space.

"Look!"

"What is that?" asked Teresa in horror. "Another rock?"

"No. It's something much worse," said Kyle gulping.

***

Reluctant to leave the spot where the capsule could return at any minute, the children and their pet dinosaur tried to build another shelter. The frightening comet was moving extremely slowly across the sky. Kyle hoped it was just a passing body and not the one that wiped out the dinosaurs. He knew the girls were thinking that, but they were afraid to say anything.

Kyle reasoned that, since the earth was still newly formed, it was probably just going through some changes. He thought that was why it seemed so unstable to him. He never read anything about all the lightning storms though.

"Kyle! Help us get this thing up and stop daydreaming."

"I wasn't daydreaming. I was thinking."

"About what?" asked Sonja.

"About how we're going to get back home. If I don't come up with an idea..." Kyle already said too much and regretted it. "I mean, I hope Dad is working on coming back for us. If we were able to get here, I'm sure Dad knows how to get here, too. He'll just get in the capsule and come back. Simple."

Sonja thought for a moment and then said, "Then why did they send a camera if they could go back themselves?"

Kyle hadn't thought about that. He didn't like what Sonja was saying.

"Yeah, Kyle. Maybe they can't come here. Did you ever stop to think about that?"

"When I went in, I didn't have a clue what the thing was for. It never crossed my mind the thing would go anywhere. I thought it was an experiment and they were filming it. Believe me, I wish we could go back before we ever went in, knowing what we know now."

"If we could get the time capsule back, why couldn't we do that anyway?"

"That would be nice. But don't you think Dad would have sent the thing back here if he had any control at all?"

The discussion was getting heated and Sonja jumped in as a peacemaker. "There's nothing we can do about it now. I think the most important thing to do is find some better place to hide and gather up some food. It looks like we might be stuck here for some time."

"Yeah. Looks like we're going to be Adam and Eve," said Kyle sarcastically.

"Great. Adam and Eve and I get stuck with my stupid brother. I guess you two will have to populate the earth."

Sonja giggled. Kyle cringed. He was into basketball and Playstations—not becoming the father of all mankind.

"No way! Nothing personal, Sonja, but I have no intention of staying here. I don't care if I have to invent and build my own time travel capsule. I'm going back. Besides, we can't produce our own children."

"Why not?" asked Sonja. She was feeling a little rejected.

"Because, then we wouldn't exist, would we? How can we come back to the past and produce ourselves in the future? You see my point? Do you see the problem?"

"I suppose you're right. If you became the father of all mankind, they'd all be butt heads," said Teresa.

"Ha. Ha. Very funny. Be serious for a minute. What are we going to do? Let's get this lean-to up and put our heads together." Kyle looked up at the comet. The girls noticed and they knew, too. "Fast, ladies."

CHAPTER TWELVE

The girls gathered up some berries and roots they had seen odd-looking dinosaurs with heads shaped like a duck eating near a stream, and they all sat down in the lean-to to eat. Sonja was delighted they didn't have to cook up any meat since she was a vegetarian. Kyle kidded her about how strange that must be—and not knowing why a doctor of animals couldn't eat meat. Not being used to the other kids, Sonja had gotten into a lengthy explanation about eating only vegetables and that she wasn't a doctor of animals like a veterinarian. Kyle kept a straight face while Teresa tried hard not to giggle.

The roots were delicious. The flavor was sweet with a hint of coconut and a texture like sponge cake. Kyle crushed some berries on his—for dessert he said. The storms had stopped and the skies cleared except for an occasional passing dark cloud.

They tried to build a fire as Kyle had seen his father do by rubbing sticks together, but the air was too moist to get a spark going. Even the flaming rock that had burst into flames went out almost immediately. The ground was too wet to sustain fire.

Kyle had warmed up to Priti. After all, he thought, he was the one that discovered the first dinosaur. When he got back to the future, he was going to be famous and make more money than Michael Jordan ever dreamed of making. Maybe he'd have him over for a little one-on-one. No doubt everyone would want to be his friend. He thought about how he would handle all the fame and fortune.

The girls had drifted off to sleep and, in time, he too slipped off into dreamland.

***

"Kyle! Wake up!"

It was Teresa. He was irritated since he was just waving to the crowds of people gathered outside his house. Cameras were flashing as he stood in the doorway. His father had finally admitted how proud he was of his son. He should have known it was a dream.

"What!"

"Something's happening! There are lights all over the sky, but we don't hear any thunder. Come see. What is it?"

Kyle jumped up and shook off his dream to see what had the girls so upset. He was shocked to see the sky filled with colorful lights that moved like walls of ribbons. He remembered reading about this and seeing pictures in books.

"It's the Northern Lights! What are they doing here? Usually you see this in the northern sky over places like Maine and New Hampshire."

The entire sky moved with the ribbons of light. It was like nothing they had ever seen. No one on earth had ever seen anything like it before or ever would again.

"What does it mean?" asked Sonja.

Kyle thought for a minute. "It has to be the comet."

"It's the one, isn't it?" asked Teresa far too calmly. "We're all going to die here with the dinosaurs."

"I don't know. I mean, I guess that's possible. The earth was hit by comets before the big one. It might just be one of those. It doesn't have to be the killer comet."

"If it is, that means that Priti is going to die, too," said Teresa sadly.

"Let's not jump to any conclusions, okay? We'll just take it as it comes." Kyle cringed when he said that. *I sound like my father.*

The earth rumbled under their feet and the volcano began to shoot fire. As it did, the sky changed before their very eyes. The light show disappeared as suddenly as it had begun. In its place, dark clouds formed as they watched. The sky became electrically charged and bolts of blue lightning streaked in every direction. The sound of thunder was so loud they could barely talk to each other.

Kyle yelled, "We have to get out of here!"

Before they could even take a step, the earth shook them into the air and they landed with a thump. As they watched, the entire horizon filled with a brilliant flash of light. The volcano responded by spewing out flames of orange and yellow lava. Kyle knew now what he dreaded all along. He was frightened more than any other time in his life. The girls were screaming and couldn't get up.

An idea popped into Kyle's mind that seemed ridiculous, but he knew if they didn't do something, they were about to become as extinct as the dinosaurs.

He yelled as loudly as he could, "Follow me!"

Teresa yelled back, "I can't get up!"

"You have to or you're going to die!"

Teresa's eyes got wide. Kyle reached down and grabbed her by the arm and yanked her up. Then he reached over and grabbed Sonja and they tried to run.

"Where are we going?" yelled Teresa.

"To the time capsule!"

Teresa thought he had lost his mind.

CHAPTER THIRTEEN

The earth shook as the giant comet smashed into the ocean—the impact sent enormous waves of water rushing away at supersonic speed. Trillions of pounds of dust and smoke belched into the air and began to immediately darken the sky. It spread out in a destructive force that had never been felt on the earth.

Anything close to the impact was vaporized on contact. The crater was the size of several U.S. states and located near the Yucatan Peninsula in the Gulf of Mexico. The comet was destroyed on impact. In several short months, every living creature on the face of the earth would die and leave a mystery for future debate. Kyle and the girls now knew the truth.

They ran as fast as their legs would take them. The spot where the capsule had been and where the distortion field still shimmered fluctuated with the electrical storm. Kyle fell on his face and tried to get up. The earth was shaking and moving under his feet like ocean waves. The girls, too, were on their knees. Teresa was calling for Priti, but the little dinosaur was long gone.

Kyle saw out of the corner of his eye something that frightened him into action. A wall of what looked like fire was heading at them with a roaring sound. He didn't know exactly what it was, but he didn't want to wait to find out. He was a hundred percent sure it meant instant death.

He pushed himself up as hard as he could and stumbled over to the girls. He shouted for them to get up, but they couldn't hear him. The sound of the thunder and the roar of the approaching wall of flames was deafening.

Half running and half falling down, Kyle pushed the girls forward. Teresa was crying. Kyle could just barely make out the area where the capsule had been. He needed to get to it or they were doomed. He hoped he was right.

As they came within a few feet, an enormous creature darted out from behind a large tree and ran at them. It was a T-Rex. Kyle wasn't sure if it was the same one, but at the moment he didn't much care.

He pushed the girls beyond the bounds of human endurance. The T-Rex ran right past them. Apparently, Kyle thought, it had more pressing things on its feeble little mind.

When they reached the distortion field, Kyle turned and saw that the wall of flames was approaching fast. He shoved Teresa and Sonja into the middle of the field and jumped in with them. He pulled the girls to the ground in the middle and squeezed as hard as he could. The wall was still coming and the roar was getting louder and louder.

***

Thirty-some years had passed since the children had left. Dr. Donavan had finally given up all hope of ever seeing his children again. He was retiring today. The building was up for sale. It had been a long lonely life. His wife had passed away ten years ago due to the grief of losing the children. She had never been the same.

He never heard from his friend, Dr. Bashan, ever again. He doubted he had had much of a life either.

Dr. David Donavan stood at the door to the vault one last time. A tear fell from his eye and splattered on the ground. Then another and another. He couldn't help himself. He decided to take one last look inside the vault. He wanted to look at the shoestring — the thread that gave him hope — just one more time.

He placed his hand against the reader and the door clicked open. *It still works.* Slowly he walked over to the distortion field and kneeled down. The shoestring was gone.

Puzzled, he stood up and scratched his head. Then he heard a sound he thought he would never hear again. It was the sound of a hundred violins in perfect harmony.

***

Kyle was sure he was about to die and braced himself for the pain. He closed his eyes and held his breath as the sound of the roaring wall of fire approached the field. Then — all was silent.

At first, Kyle thought he was dead. He thought that maybe death was greatly feared for nothing. Then he saw the reason for the sudden silence. They were inside the time capsule!

Kyle shook the girls and they opened their eyes. All around them was the green gel protecting them from the wall of fire that had descended upon them. The gel was moving. Slowly at first. Then they heard it — the sound of a hundred violins in perfect harmony. To the three children, it was the sweetest sound they had ever heard.

Teresa looked down when something caught her eye. It was her shoestring. She quickly picked it up and tied it back on her sneaker.

Kyle smiled at his little sister. She had unknowingly saved all their lives.

***

Dr. Donavan watched with eager hope that maybe, just maybe, his children had come back. They would all be older now. Much older. He watched as the gel appeared in the distortion field. Inside he could see three figures. They still looked young. He thought that was odd.

The sound of the music grew louder and louder. The pitch went higher and higher. It was so deafening, Dr. Donavan raised his hands to his ears. He thought his eardrums were going to explode.

And then—everything ceased to exist.

CHAPTER FOURTEEN

The children watched as the walls spun faster and faster. The sound of the violins rose in volume and pitch. Then it shimmered and turned clear like water. Finally it pulsated with all the colors of the rainbow.

They grabbed their ears, but this time they couldn't take their eyes off the spinning liquid. For a brief second, Kyle thought he saw the face of an old man watching them through the spinning walls. Then it was gone. He thought he must have imagined it.

When the sound got so loud they thought they were going to die, it stopped. The walls had returned to a solid green gel.

"Is everyone okay?"

"Yeah..." said a stunned Teresa.

"Look!" said Sonja. "The camera is still right in the middle of the capsule."

Kyle examined it. "It hasn't even started to run. I think we need to get out of here. Right now!"

After what they had been through, the girls didn't need any coaxing. First Teresa, then Sonja, and finally Kyle slipped through the gel and stood on the other side. They were home.

***

"Okay, Paul, ready for launch. Is the camera set to auto?"

"Yes, David. I set it myself. Launch sequence initiated. Harmonics set to 50%."

"Once we launch, we better get back and check on the children. If I know my son, he won't sit still for long. Thanks for letting me know the capsule returned. It was, what...twenty days, right?"

"Correct, Dr. David. You really think the image is a dinosaur?"

"Either that, or a zoo with very strange animals. It was hard to tell through the gel. Something was there, that's for sure. There's no way to tell how far back it went. It could be anytime. Any time, but not any place. The capsule can't move. It should be right where it is now, but it emerged somewhere in time."

"Essentially correct. I guess we'll never know until we send a human. But we don't know...we just don't know if they'll survive."

***

Kyle stood back as the sound of a hundred violins filled the air. Somehow they had arrived back in time. While he didn't understand the science behind it, Teresa's shoestring had provided the means for the capsule to return.

"Now what? Dad's going to ground us, you know. How are we going to explain where we were?"

"Look, butthead. We almost got ourselves killed and all you can worry about..."

"Hey!" Sonja interrupted Kyle. "Look at your clothes!"

"What about my clo..." Kyle looked at Teresa with his mouth open. "You're...not dirty!"

"Huh?"

"Sonja's right. You're not...none of us are dirty. When we got in the capsule, we were covered in dirt! Now...we're not. What on earth...?"

"How can that be?" asked Teresa.

The sound of the violins grew louder and louder. The walls of the capsule began to move.

"What if we...came back before we left?" said Sonja.

"Have you gone out of your mind?"

"No. Wait a minute. Sonja may be right."

"Right? We came back before we left? What kind of stupid idea is that?"

"Okay, you explain to me how your clothes look like you never left."

Teresa thought for a moment and realized that there was no explanation, at least no explanation that made any sense. "If that's true..."

"Then we need to get out of here as quickly as possible! Come on!"

Teresa and Sonja went through the door of the vault and out into the laboratory. Kyle turned to take one last look and marvel at his experience. Then he, too, went out and shut the door.

As he crossed the laboratory to leave and follow the girls, he heard the sound of an elevator door open. Quickly he raced across the lab before his father caught him.

***

"I cannot wait to see the film when it returns this time," said Dr. Bashan. "Maybe we will get a better image?"

"I hope so. Let's go check on the kids. If I know Kyle he's probably gotten into some kind of trouble. That kid will never amount to anything, I'm afraid. He has no focus."

"I know what you mean. My little Sonja is bright, but she has no sense of adventure. I had to drag her out of the house today so she wouldn't just sit on the couch and read."

"Hey, I have an idea. Maybe we can take them to the museum. Think they'd like to see some dinosaur bones?"

Kyle shut the door very carefully so as not to make a sound. He snickered to himself as he ran across the hall to where the girls were anxiously waiting for him.

CHAPTER FIFTEEN

Kyle, Teresa and Sonja stood in front of the strange looking skeleton of a dinosaur. The pictures that depicted the animal were all wrong. It was called a Bambisaurus and the sign said it was a member of the Velociraptor family. Kyle was irritated and walked over to one of the museum guides.

"Excuse me, sir. This exhibit over here?"

"Yes. A fine example of the species. Only one of its kind ever found. Very nasty beast. Flesh-eater..."

"I'm afraid that's not true. This animal ate roots and berries and was very friendly. I think you need to change the sign..."

The guide began chuckling. He was an older man with a bald head and a bit of a paunch that hung out over his belt. "Now, how would you know that, young man?"

Kyle hated to be treated like a little kid and this man was beginning to irritate him.

"Because I was there!" he shot back without thinking.

The man laughed louder and his belly vibrated.

"Oh, hah, ha! Wait until I tell the professor about this one. Ha, ha! That's rich. He was there! Ha, ha, ha!"

Kyle stormed away and rejoined the girls.

"Guess he didn't believe you?" asked Sonja.

"No. We have no way of proving it."

Kyle noticed that Teresa was crying.

"What's the matter?"

"Kyle, Priti's probably dead, isn't she?"

"Of course she's dead. All the dinosaurs are dead. They died 65 million years ago. Remember?"

Teresa wiped her eyes and looked directly at Kyle. "We have to go back."

Without a beat, Kyle answered, "You're right. We do have to go back."

PART II

THE RAPTORS

CHAPTER SIXTEEN

Kyle sat on the edge of his bed and listened intently with his eyes closed to the music coming through the earphones. He wasn't bopping to the beat—it was far too complicated for that. In fact, the expression on his face was that of someone enduring a great deal of pain. It wasn't painful. Kyle was simply concentrating—concentrating harder than he ever had in his life. He knew he was onto something, but he wasn't quite sure what. He knew the shoestring left in the time capsule by his sister Teresa was the key to figuring it all out. Yet, it eluded him. The answer was just beyond his ability to comprehend—to understand a theory so complex, so deep, that only a few men understood its implications. His father was one of them.

***

Teresa knocked on his door again—harder this time. "Kyle, Mom wants you! You have to take out the garbage! Kyle!"

She knocked again and again, pounding the door with her fist. Frustrated, Teresa ignored the sign on the door written in red magic marker that said, "DO NOT ENTER UNDER PENALTY OF DEATH—ESPECIALLY GIRLS!" and she turned the doorknob. She was surprised it hadn't been locked. It was very un-Kyle-like. She stood in front of Kyle with her hands on her hips and was about to yell when she noticed the expression on his face.

What is he listening to? She wondered if her brother had finally lost what little of his mind was left. *Maybe the time capsule stole his brain—or left it back in time.* She shook off the thought since it reminded her that Priti, the bambiraptor, had probably died when the comet struck. *Of course it died*, she thought. *It was 65 million years ago! How stupid of me.*

Teresa reached over and gave her brother a shove on the shoulder and he practically flew off the bed. The earphones jerked from his head and he wound up on the floor.

"What in the world are you doing? Are you out of your mind?"

"No, but I think you are. What are you listening to anyway?"

Kyle quickly reached over and shut off the CD player.

"Are you listening to rap again? Dad will kill you if he finds out."

"It's none of your...hey, what are you doing in my room?"

"Mom wants you to take out the garbage, lazy head."

"You came in here for that? She thinks the whole world will end if the garbage doesn't go out on time. What's the big deal? Why don't you take out the garbage for a change?"

"That's your job. I'm going to the mall with Sonja today."

"Sonja? I thought her mother wouldn't let her near that place of demons."

"Her mother thinks I am a very nice girl."

"Well…what she doesn't know will hurt her. Now, get out of my room!"

Kyle accidentally hit the eject button while fiddling with the CD player and Teresa got a glimpse of the disk: "Mendelssohn for Strings, Opus 75." He quickly pulled the disk out and slipped it under his pillow. Teresa was so stunned she was speechless. Kyle knew she saw it and turned bright red.

"Now I know you've lost your mind," she finally managed before turning and walking out the door. In the hallway she scratched her head and wondered what Kyle was up to. Then she remembered the sound of the time capsule: the sound of a hundred violins in perfect harmony.

***

Dr. Bashan sat at the computer and entered the complex instructions as Dr. Donavan watched in astonishment. He couldn't understand how anyone could keep so many numbered sequences in his head without making a mistake.

"Well, Dr. David, I have made the minor adjustments to the code. The harmonics are the same as before, except for the super high frequencies. I adjusted them plus .002%. According to your theory, that should send the capsule back further in time."

"It's still just a guess. We're playing with something no one ever thought was even possible. If we can get a rough calculation of how far back we sent the capsule, we'll better be able to control it."

As physicists, the two doctors had stumbled across a secret that helped them unravel the mysteries of the universe. At one time scientists thought that atoms were the smallest particles in the universe. Then they discovered even smaller particles that made up all the parts of the atoms: the electrons, protons and neutrons. But then sub-atomic particles were found that made up these smaller particles. However, even Einstein might have been surprised that the sub-atomic particles contained little bits of electricity that pulsated like tiny ribbons or strings.

What Dr. David Donavan and Dr. Paul Bashan discovered was that they could change the way the strings act by bombarding them with sound. What one could hear sounded like violins — a hundred of them. But the sounds had to be perfectly tuned beyond what the human ear could hear. It was the sound that couldn't be heard, because they were too high or too low, that caused the capsule they created to move through what some called the *space-time continuum*. In effect, they had actually created a time machine. It was no longer science fiction.

What they didn't know was the power they had unleashed on an unsuspecting world — and that their children were the only ones that could save the universe from extinction.

CHAPTER SEVENTEEN

Teresa and Sonja laughed at the boys flirting with them. They seemed so silly and immature.

"My mother would sweat in her *sari* if she were here."

"Her what?" asked Teresa.

"Her Indian dress. She wanted me to wear one today. I told her I'd stand out like a sore finger."

"Sore thumb."

"What?"

"The correct word is thumb. You'd stand out like a sore thumb."

"Oh. You see what I have to put up with? Is your mother so protective?"

"Yeah. But I guess not as bad as your mother. I suppose they just care."

"Yes, they do love us, don't they?"

"It's not like we'd get in trouble or anything...unless Kyle were with us."

"Yes, Kyle," said Sonja with a sigh.

"You don't really like my brother, do you?"

Sonja had a sheepish look on her face. "Well, he is very smart."

"How can you say that when he almost got us killed?"

"He got us back, didn't he? I doubt anyone could have figured that out."

"That reminds me, I caught him listening to classical music today!"

"So? Is that bad? I like classical music."

"But this is Kyle we're talking about. Kyle always listens to rap. Nothing else. I think he's lost his mind."

Sonja stopped walking and looked at Teresa. "He wasn't listening to violin music, was he?"

Astonished, Teresa answered, "Yes. How did you…?"

"He's trying to figure out how to get back."

Teresa's jaw dropped. "Oh my god! We can't go back in that…thing. We were almost killed the last time. What if my dad catches us?"

"What about Priti?"

Teresa paused as her mind raced back in time — 65 million years ago. She thought about the little dinosaur they had adopted or, rather, that had adopted them. "Do you think we can really save her? Why would Kyle want to do that, anyway? He didn't even like her."

"I think Kyle wants to prove something. I think he wants to bring Priti back with us."

"Oh my god! Really?"

"I'll bet that's why he's listening to the violins. He wants to figure out how to make the capsule go back far enough to rescue her. Besides, I think he kind of warmed up to Priti." Sonja's eyes sparkled.

"Oh, please! Let's just do some shopping. I have to spend some money or I'm going to vomit!"

***

"Dad? Can I ask you some questions?"

"Make it quick. I'm in a hurry."

"You work in string theory, don't you?"

Dr. Donavan was startled by the question. "Yes...yes I do."

"Could you explain to me how that works?"

Dr. Donavan stood with his mouth open for several seconds. Then he began chuckling to himself. "Ha, ha! That's good. You really had me there for a moment. I've got to go. Don't you have some homework to do? String theory...oh that's rich! Ha, ha."

Kyle stood in the doorway as his father walked into the garage and got into his car. He heard the sound of the engine turn and, in a split second, the BMW roared to life. Kyle was fuming as he watched the car move slowly through the garage door. The sound of the diesel engine hurt his ears and the smell of the exhaust made him feel ill.

Hurt, he went back to his room and put the earphones back on. Soon, he was lost in the sounds of the violins as they reached a *crescendo* — a high point in the music. He was surprised that it made him feel good. A tingle ran across his head as if electricity were being released in his brain. He wondered, *Could there be a connection between the sounds — the harmonics that sounded like violins — and the sound of music? Was that the key to string theory?*

He pondered the sound of the BMW's engine. It had hurt his ears. It wasn't harmonious. It was disruptive. Maybe the key to string theory had to do with the pitch being perfectly tuned at every octave and every note in between.

Kyle looked over at his dog sitting at the edge of the bed. The little min-pin's ears were twitching. The miniature pincher had the same coloring as a Doberman pincher, but they weren't the same dog— not even close. Kyle remembered the nervous little bambiraptor. It had reminded him of his dog. Toby was reacting to something he was hearing. Was the dog hearing sound in the music that he couldn't? Could Toby hear the violins through the earphones? Another thought occurred to him. *Maybe it's what I can't hear that's really the key. Can't animals hear sounds humans can't?*

The more he thought about it, the more frustrated he became. Maybe one of his science teachers would know. He didn't need his father. He'd figure this out, go back in the capsule and bring the bambiraptor back with him. He'd show him he wasn't as dumb as everyone thought he was!

***

It was 12:00 midnight and everyone in the house was asleep. Kyle dressed quietly and tiptoed out of the bedroom, down the stairs to the front foyer and then shined his flashlight on the keypad to the house security system. His father's fingerprints had permanently smudged the numbers and it was a simple matter for Kyle to deduce the exact sequence: 122448. It was his father's birthday. His father was too predictable and Kyle chuckled.

He opened the door and reset the alarm. Then he disappeared behind the house and climbed over the fence to the neighbor's yard. Two eyes peered out from behind the small opening to the doghouse. They were evil looking. A low growl came rolling out and across the ground that would have scared anyone—anyone but Kyle.

"Godzilla," he whispered. "Come 'ere boy, come on. I've got a *cookie* for you." The strong accent on the word "cookie" was a signal for the two hundred pound rotweiler. Godzilla stopped growling and began lapping at his lips sending saliva spraying in every direction. The massive dog approached Kyle with his head down and nuzzled his armpit.

"Here 'ya go, boy. Good dog!" Kyle gave Godzilla a couple of big dog treats and then continued his journey. He needed to get to the lab and it was a long walk through many yards in the black of night. Somehow, after his journey back in time to the land of the dinosaurs, nothing in this time period seemed as frightening—except maybe math class.

Once Kyle arrived at the lab, he took his father's keys out and turned the lock until he heard a loud clicking sound. Then he typed in the code—same one: 122448 and went in. The keypad to the laboratory door itself was different, but he remembered from before and punched in the sequence. The door clicked open.

Bypassing the large, safe-like door that housed the time capsule, Kyle headed for the main computer station on the second floor. He walked past the other computers that were networked to the mainframe upstairs. He knew he had to get to the master control panel in order to initiate the program.

When he got to the end of the computers and all the tubes that still glowed light green running throughout the ceiling and walls, he came to the first real obstacle of the night: the elevator. He shined his flashlight across the keypad to make the fingerprints more visible. There were smudges present, but they didn't add up to his father's birthday this time. Kyle cringed. What if they were Dr. Bashan's birthday? What would he do then, he wondered.

A wave of nervousness threatened to scare him out of the building altogether. *Okay, calm down. Think! What do the numbers mean? I hate math...*

He thought of his mother's birthday. No. They were the wrong numbers. Teresa? *Yes! It's Teresa's birthday!* He keyed in the sequence. It didn't work. What could be wrong? *Maybe backwards? Is my father getting crafty in his old age?*

Kyle keyed the numbers in backwards. Still it didn't work. Now he was starting to sweat. If he got it wrong the third time, the alarm would go off automatically. He only had one more shot and one more idea. It either had to be Teresa's birthday forward—then backward—or the opposite. Most people would enter it forward first. But what if his father was being clever?

Kyle punched in the numbers and held his breath—forward, then backward. The elevator came to life and the door opened.

I always knew they liked her best!

***

Dr. Donavan awoke and tried to fluff his pillow and get back to sleep. He pulled the blanket up over his head and curled up like a baby, but it was no use. He couldn't sleep. It bothered him that he had been so abrupt with Kyle. His mind wouldn't let him forget it.

He had to admit he had been short with him. Maybe Kyle really did care about string theory, he thought. *Maybe I just crushed the one thing that could wake the young boy up and get him to think seriously about his life.*

Dr. Donavan got out of bed and headed downstairs for a glass of milk. He opened the refrigerator door. In the distance, he could hear the neighbor's dog barking. Then he had an idea. Maybe he'd go up and get Kyle out of bed and apologize. Maybe Kyle would want a glass of milk? He turned and headed for the stairway.

CHAPTER EIGHTEEN

Kyle entered the upstairs laboratory from the elevator and was stunned by the view of hundreds of computers all linked to three screens situated on a console. There were banks of hard drives on shelves that ran the length of the room. Only a single purple light lit the room and gave it an eerie glow. He could smell the ozone—like a thunderstorm had just occurred.

Cautiously, he walked over to the first station and sat down. The screen was black. He moved the mouse and it jumped to life immediately.

"Wow! This is fast!"

Several icons were visible on the screen off to one side and the bars were clearly Microsoft Windows. He thought he could handle it.

First, he scrolled over to the programs file and up popped a long list. He didn't recognize any of the names, so he moved the mouse off and the list disappeared. He tried one of the icons. It was a green glowing circle with a skull and crossbones in the center. He double clicked the mouse and up popped a log-on window. He hadn't figured on it being protected with a password. He decided to try a name— Teresa—his father's favorite child. Up popped a warning: "Invalid Password. Please Make Sure the Caps Button is OFF and Try Again."

Kyle thought. Maybe his mother: Medina. He typed in his mother's name. Same result. He tried their names frontward and backwards, the name of the dog, the mailman, his father's name, his grandmother's—on both sides—then grandfather's and even the neighbor's dog. He knew there wouldn't be any danger of setting off an alarm like on the security system, but he was wasting time. It had taken him an hour to get there and another half hour to get upstairs into the lab.

Finally, out of sheer frustration, he typed in K-y-l-e. "Password Accepted."

You've got to be kidding!

Then the screen came to life with thousands— maybe millions of numbers scrolling across. The banks of computers all came on simultaneously. He could see the lights on every one of them blinking rapidly as data was being processed.

The whirring and clicking noises went on for what seemed like an eternity, but took no more than two minutes. Then everything became quiet and the screen went blank again. Kyle's heart sank. He knew he only had a few more minutes before he would have to go back home and try again tomorrow night.

Then, without any warning the fluid in the tubes began to move. Slowly at first. And then more quickly. And then it stopped as quickly as it had begun. Kyle wondered if he had accidentally hit the keyboard, but his hands were rigid and frozen to the side of the console in fear. He looked at the computer screen and a small window had popped up. It said: "Do you want to initiate new program changes?"

Kyle thought a minute. He wondered whether his father and Dr. Bashan had made corrections in the program. Considering the overwhelming task of trying to figure out the millions—maybe billions if not trillions of bits of information that had scrolled across the screen earlier, Kyle decided to go ahead and hit the "enter" key. Another window popped up with a bar. It was filling from left to right. Below it said "15 minutes to launch."

Kyle brought both his hands to his face and screamed: "Yikes! I've just launched the time capsule!"

Frantic, he hit the "delete" key. Nothing. The "escape" key. Still nothing. It seemed there was no way to stop the launch. Kyle ran back to the elevator. It was closed. He had to punch in the password all over again. The first time it didn't work. He was so nervous, he mis-keyed one of the numbers. He tried to breath slowly to calm himself. Then he entered the code again. The elevator had gone to the bottom floor. Fear rushed through his body. Had his father called the elevator? Was he coming up now? *He'll kill me!*

***

Teresa heard someone walking up the staircase. She thought it might be Kyle.

She ran to the door and swung it open hoping to scare him. Instead, she scared her father half to death. He spilled a glass of milk all over the rug.

"Dad? Why are you walking around in the middle of the night with a glass of milk?"

"Why did you try and scare me? Look at this mess! Your mom is going to have a canary."

"I thought you were Kyle."

"Why? Does he usually walk around in the middle of the night?"

"No. Well…maybe lately."

"Why? Has there been something bothering him?"

"Uh...no...not really. Gotta go. I need to get my beauty sleep. Night, Dad."

Dr. Donavan went into the adjoining bathroom for a towel and some detergent to clean up the milk. When he was done, he decided it would be best if he waited until morning to talk to Kyle.

***

Kyle stood outside the capsule as the sound of the violins grew faintly in the background. He considered his options nervously. If he decided not to go, his father would find out what he had done and ground him for the rest of his life. If he went in and took the trip back, he didn't know if he'd be able to figure out how to get back to the present. He remembered that the computer screen had said something about a new program, but did that mean someone had changed the destination?

The sound of the violins increased. He would have to make his decision now — or it would be made for him. Kyle pushed on the green gel and it parted. Once inside, he quickly untied one of his sneakers and placed the shoestring in the opening — half in — half out. No sooner had he done that than the gel began to move.

Kyle watched the gel swirl with awe as the violins increased in pitch and volume. The gel began to move faster and faster as all of the colors of the rainbow pulsed up and down. The sound became almost deafening, but Kyle refused to hold his ears this time. He wanted to understand what was going on and didn't want to miss anything. The gel turned blue and then appeared to change into a pure liquid — like water. The music filled his ears and his mind. Faster and faster, louder and louder until he felt he was going to burst and then…silence. The gel returned to its green color and consistency. It was now solid.

Kyle had gone somewhere, but he wasn't sure where. All was quiet outside the capsule unlike the previous trip. There were no sounds of thunder and lightning—no sounds of any kind. It was eerily quiet.

Kyle felt surprisingly exhilarated. It was as if he had just been on the octopus ride at the carnival. It was that kind of a rush—only more. His mind felt clear and sharp. He even had the unusual thought that he could do math. And that without feeling ill.

He decided to venture out of the capsule after waiting a few minutes for the sound of approaching apatasaurs. Checking to make sure the shoestring was still half in and half out of the capsule first, he then went through the opening. No sooner had he gone through than the capsule started to spin again. The sound of the violins filled his mind with its soothing music. He no longer felt the need to hold his ears. It made him feel good.

When the capsule was gone, Kyle turned to see where he was. He inhaled sharply at the sight of what was waiting for him.

CHAPTER NINETEEN

It was 5:00 AM and Dr. Donavan rubbed his eyes. The sun was glaring through the morning window and it was painful. Medina, his wife, was up long before him and making breakfast. Teresa helped by making the coffee, while her mom scrambled the eggs and started the sausages. This was a family that loved to eat breakfast. It was the only meal of the day all of them could get together.

"Where's Kyle?" asked Dr. Donavan.

"Probably still asleep," said Medina. "Teresa, why don't you go and knock on his door."

The invitation to wake Kyle from a deep sleep was too tempting for Teresa to pass up. "Why, sure Mom! I'd be happy to do that!"

"Now, don't get fresh, Teresa. Don't start a fight so early in the morning. Just knock on his door and tell him it's time to eat."

"O...kay," said Teresa dejectedly.

She bounded up the stairs and ran up to Kyle's door and listened. She could hear Toby scratching at the door and whimpering to be let out. Teresa knocked loudly. "Kyle! Time to eat! Mom said you have to come! NOW!"

She listened, but all she could hear was Toby barking and running in circles obviously anxious to get out. She tried again, but no response from Kyle.

Maybe he's listening to that music again with the earphones on.

She decided to try the door handle. It was open. Toby came flying out of the room and down the stairs like a rocket. She could see the outline of Kyle in bed. He was still asleep.

"Kyle! Wake up!"

There was no movement. Concerned, she went over to the bed and shook him. He felt soft.

"What on earth?"

Teresa pulled the covers back. "Oh my god! He's gone!"

Quickly she pulled the covers back up and over the pillows Kyle had piled on the bed. She didn't know what to do. Her first impulse was to run downstairs and tell her parents. Then she wondered if Kyle had decided to go back without her and get Priti.

***

"Did you wake him?"

"He's still asleep, Dad. Says he…uh…doesn't feel well and just needs some extra rest. He says he'll get up later."

Dr. Donavan thought about it for a minute and then said, "Okay. Let him sleep awhile. I'll talk to him when I get home."

"If Kyle isn't feeling well, maybe I should check on him," said her mom as she picked up the cloth from the sink and wiped her hands.

"No! I mean…you don't want to wake him…uh…just yet, Mom. He really, really wants to just sleep some more."

Now her mom became even more concerned and raced up the stairs. Teresa covered her ears.

"David!" came the scream from the top of the stairs. "Kyle's gone! He's run away!"

***

"This is my fault. I shouldn't have been so hard on him yesterday."

"What do you mean, dear? How is this your fault?"

"Kyle wanted to know about my work...with string theory. I thought he was just being his usual self. You know...a wise guy. But he must have been serious. Teresa, do you know what Kyle's up to?"

"I...uh...know he's been listening to classical music. Maybe he's going insane?" she said with a half-hearted smile.

"Kyle? Listening to...classical music?" said her mother. "That is odd."

"Well, maybe not," said Dr. Donavan. "What kind of classical was Kyle listening to, Teresa? Do you know?"

"Not really. I wouldn't be caught dead listening to that stuff. All those violins make me ill."

"Violins?" said her father alarmed. "Kyle has been listening to *violin music*?" He stood up and walked around the room deep in thought while Teresa hoped her father wouldn't figure it out. Her mother sat there with a puzzled look on her face.

"Did Kyle go near the lab the other day when you kids were in the break room?"

"Uh...I don't know."

"Did he leave the break room?"

Teresa knew that they had come back in time before they left and her father couldn't know they were in the lab. "He went out and looked in there. Then he came back."

Dr. Donavan wasn't convinced. He knew his daughter well enough to know she was hiding something. She had just tried to cover for her brother and now she was acting evasive in her answers.

"Medina, I'm going to the lab. Don't call the police just yet. Let me check on something. Teresa, get dressed. You're coming with me."

Teresa had a sinking feeling in her heart.

CHAPTER TWENTY

Kyle turned to run back into the capsule even though he knew it was gone. Fear racked his body. He wanted to run, but instinctively knew it would be the wrong thing to do. Staring at him were seven vicious looking raptors — velociraptors — just like the ones in Jurassic Park. He remembered the animals in the movie. They had been highly intelligent creatures with an unquenchable thirst for human flesh.

These animals appeared more curious than aggressive. They were bobbing their heads up and down and licking the air — trying to taste him to see if he was, in fact, edible. They were much larger than Priti. The talons on their front paws were indeed longer and more menacing in appearance. But they didn't act like they were ready to pounce on him. At least not yet.

Kyle decided the best defense was a quick offense. He guessed that they would begin to posture before they pounced and by that time it would be too late. He needed to forget the movie and remember that this was reality. He remembered what the man at the museum had said about bambiraptors — that they were carnivorous flesh-eaters. It wasn't true. Kyle decided to treat the velociraptors just like any aggressive animal.

Kyle ran right up to the closest animal and screamed at it. At the same time he smacked it across the face. The response was immediate. They backed down and ran away from him.

"Get out of here you skuzzy-looking stupid toads! Or I'll pull the gizzards out of your throats."

The raptors were buying the tough guy image at the moment, but they hadn't been scared off. They kept their distance and began spreading out while licking the air and bobbing their heads again. They were still thinking about eating him, apparently.

Kyle looked around and found a branch hanging low off a tree and snapped it off. He felt safer with a weapon.

Looking around, he saw that he was in the same exact spot they had traveled to the last time, but he deduced it was earlier in time. It was before the comet had hit but he wasn't sure how long. The vegetation looked a little different. It was sparser and the air wasn't quite as humid. It still smelled like sulfur, but not as strong. In the distance where the volcano had been there was nothing. He could see movement beyond that, but he couldn't tell what it was. He also knew that he couldn't bring back a velociraptor to the future. He was uncomfortable enough with Priti. He wondered if he had gone back too far and Priti hadn't been born yet.

Kyle checked the spot where the capsule had been and made sure the shoestring was still visible. Half of it was and the other half was gone. When he reached down for it, his hand went right through as if it wasn't there. He heard a sound behind him—a cracking twig.

He turned and saw that the raptors were no longer bobbing their heads. They had assumed a menacing stance and were advancing toward him all at the same time. Kyle could picture them ripping him to pieces and fighting over his arms and legs. He decided that he had had enough. It was the wrong idea to go back in time. He jumped into the middle of the capsule's distortion field as he had done the last time and waited for the soothing sounds of the violins. He heard nothing. It hadn't worked. The raptors were hissing now with their heads held low and jaws open revealing a mouthful of razor sharp teeth. Kyle had never been so frightened in his life. He thought this was much worse than the first time when the comet had hit.

***

Dr. Donavan met his partner Dr. Paul Bashan and his daughter Sonja at the entrance to the lab. Teresa gave a quick look at Sonja and tried to convey what was going on without saying anything about what had happened. She needn't have.

"Teresa, Sonja, you stay here in the lounge and don't leave! We'll be right back."

Dr. Donavan slammed the door and stormed off toward the main lab with Dr. Bashan.

"What's going on?" asked Sonja with grave concern in her voice.

"It's my brother again."

"Kyle? Is he okay?"

"I don't know. He wasn't in his bed this morning. He didn't say anything to me, but he's been acting funny lately."

"Do you think he went back in time without us?"

"Oh my god! I hope not. If he did, we may have to explain what happened."

"They'd never believe us if we did. Oh, Teresa, what if Kyle can't get back? Remember all those dangerous creatures? And the comet? Suppose he doesn't get back in the capsule again?"

"Let's not get too anxious until we know for sure he's…gone." Tears welled up in Teresa's eyes and that had the same effect on Sonja. Both girls began to cry and hug each other.

***

The two doctors emerged from the elevator and were startled to see all the computers up and running. The program report was scrolling down the screen on the main computer and it read: "Launch Sequence Initiated…time in transit…4 hrs…11 minutes…36 seconds."

Dr. Bashan looked at his watch. "The capsule left at approximately…3:00 A.M. How did your son figure this out? He couldn't have done it alone. David, it took me years before I could handle this program. I refuse to believe some young teenager, no offense…figured out how to launch the capsule."

"This is all my fault. If I had paid attention to him…"

"What do you mean?"

"Yesterday Kyle asked me about string theory. I thought he was just pulling my leg…you know…being the smart-alecky kid he always is. Apparently, he was taking this far more seriously than I thought. If I had gone to his room last night and tried to awaken him, I would have prevented this from happening."

"It is always clearer when you look back. What is it you say in this country: 'Hind sight is 20-20?'"

"You're right. Now we have to figure out how to get him back. Can you intervene in the program and initiate a recall?"

"I don't think we can do that. We have to wait until the capsule comes back on its own. The harmonics must fade slowly until it reappears. The last time we launched it was quite some time before it came back with the tape."

"You reset the harmonics to go back a little further this time. Can you tell if Kyle altered the program? Do you have any way of knowing how far back you might have sent him?"

"It was just a wild guess. We need many more launches to correlate the film with the time period. It will always go back to the same place, but not necessarily the same time. There was no camera in the capsule this time."

"Kyle's shoestring was half in and half out of the machine. We know he went back. *I have to get my son back!*" Tears began to pour from Dr. Donavan's eyes. Dr. Bashan put his arm around his shoulder. It wasn't something he was comfortable doing, but he was touched by the love David had for his son and felt the pain by imagining how he would feel if Sonja had gone with him.

They were startled when the sound of violins filled the air. The capsule was returning.

CHAPTER TWENTY-ONE

Kyle raised the stick and tried to look as scary as he could. He was still trying to bluff his way out. It was an act of desperation. The situation seemed hopeless. He was outnumbered and any one of these creatures was capable of ripping him to shreds in a matter of seconds.

One of the raptors advanced boldly toward Kyle. It was the one he had struck. Kyle was wishing he had opted for the friendly approach, but it was clearly too late now. The raptor lunged and snapped at Kyle but seemed reluctant to go beyond the distortion field. Kyle had little confidence it would just sit there and wait for him. He closed his eyes and swung the stick with all his might. Swooooosh! Nothing but air. Opening his eyes and expecting to see the raptor lunging, Kyle was surprised to see all of them fleeing down the hill toward the valley below as quickly as they could run.

"Well, I guess that scared them!"

Kyle thought he heard something breathing behind him. He turned and stared at two muscular and powerful scaly legs with large claws on the end of each toe—three on each foot. The old saying his mother used to say came to mind: "Out of the pan and into the fire."

Kyle looked down at the puny stick he was holding. It was going to be of little use against this creature. There was no way he was going to bluff his way out. He started to turn and run but something about the T-Rex changed his mind. It wasn't even looking at him. The animal had its eyes on the fleeing raptors.

Without warning, the towering monster leaped into the air right toward Kyle, who dove to the ground as one massive foot came crashing down mere inches from his head. Had he ducked even a fraction of an inch the wrong way, he would have been flattened like a pancake.

Kyle lay there for several minutes taking short jerky breaths. He couldn't believe he was alive. Sweat poured down his face and into his armpits. He slowly stood up and watched as the T-Rex caught up with one of the raptors and began shaking it violently from side to side; he realized he had also just peed his pants. He decided that it wouldn't be a good thing to remain where he was but he also didn't want to venture too far from the distortion field in case the capsule returned.

***

Not far from the embankment where he could see the clearing near the distortion field, Kyle found a large pond. It was murky and dark and had a peculiar odor. A light breeze blew across the surface rippling the pond with small waves. The sky was relatively clear with what appeared to be a thin haze that glistened with orange and purple. The sun shone brightly directly overhead. It didn't seem as bright through the haze as normal. Kyle knew from past experience that nothing about this time period was what he expected.

Rather than going in the water, Kyle undressed and rinsed his pants off. He was glad the girls hadn't joined him this time. He would never live it down.

Above the breeze making rustling noises through the trees, he could hear all manner of sounds—the sounds of dinosaurs! Forgetting the close encounter he had just had, Kyle felt himself calming and even becoming a little excited about being there. His mind never felt so clear. He remembered it seemed to come as he listened to the sounds of the harmonics so perfectly balanced. Not even the violin music he had been listening to recently had managed to move him so much. It was as if it had reached down into his very being and massaged his brain and heart.

Still he couldn't shake the nagging feeling that it meant something—something more than just the sound. He knew it had to do with string theory, but what? More than anything else at that moment he had the urge to understand how the universe worked. He wanted to know how he was able to go back in time and how he was able to arrive before he had left the last time. He also hoped he would be able to accomplish that feat again. If not, he was going to get seriously grounded. Maybe his father would ground him for a million years. He certainly had the ability to do that with the time capsule. It was a scary thought.

The breeze stopped and the trees became quiet. Even the water flattened out and looked like glass. He looked down into the water and stared at himself. At least that's what he thought. Then the eyes that were staring back disappeared with a ripple. He felt like his blood had just turned cold in his body.

***

The girls obediently followed their fathers as they led the way into the lab. They walked past the desk where Kyle had retrieved the glove and used it to get into the vault containing the time capsule. Dr. Donavan entered the code and the vault door slowly began to swing open. Inside the girls could see the capsule. They looked at each other hopefully.

"Have you ever seen this before?"

Rather than answer her father, Teresa asked, "Where...where's Kyle? Is he in there?"

"No. He's not and I'm very concerned. If he went in this...machine, he might never be back."

Teresa burst into tears. Sonja grabbed her face and tried to hold back, but not very successfully.

Horrified, Dr. Donavan and Dr. Bashan looked at each other dumbfounded.

"Sonja," said her father softly, "you must tell me everything you know. It is a matter of life and death for young Kyle."

Sonja responded by bolting from the room. Dr. Donavan reached out and grabbed Teresa's arm before she could run, too. "Teresa, I found a shoestring belonging to your brother sticking half in and half out of the machine when it returned. This is very serious and I'm sorry if it upsets you, but we have to act now to rescue Kyle...or we may never see him again."

Teresa wiped the tears from her eyes and looked down at the shoestring. She shook her head and managed a small smile. "Kyle will be back. The shoestring is the key, although I don't know why. The last time..."

"Last time! What last time? What are you talking about?"

"You'd never believe me anyway even if I told you."

"Told me what?"

"That we went back in time before."

All of them sat in the lounge at the laboratory: Teresa, her father and her mother as well as Sonja and both of her parents. The two of them had just recounted the story of their trip back in time. A look of disbelief peppered with uncertainty was etched on the faces of the parents.

"This doesn't make a bit of sense!" Teresa's mother remarked strongly. "If you went back in time, we'd know it. Why are you making this up? What are you hiding?"

Sonja's mother Ravina said, "Actually, it might be true. There are things about the universe that even we scientists don't have all the answers to."

"How did you know you came back in time before you left?" asked Dr. Donavan.

Teresa answered, "We knew it when we looked at each other. We were filthy and covered with mud and dirt when we left. But when we came out of the capsule, we were clean again. I even found my shoestring…"

"Shoestring? Again with the shoestring. What do you mean when you say you lost your shoestring?"

"I lost it when we got in the capsule the first time. Kyle tried to get it out, but it was like it wasn't there. I know that sounds weird, but isn't Kyle's shoestring in the capsule this time? Even after it returned without him?"

"What do you think this…shoestring means, Sonja?" asked Dr. Bashan.

"We…Teresa and I didn't have a clue. But Kyle did. He didn't explain it to us, but he seemed to think it was responsible for the capsule returning once we entered the distortion field."

The two doctors looked at each other with raised eyebrows. It didn't escape their notice that Sonja had referred to a phenomenon that only they, out of all the scientists in the world, had ever witnessed before.

"You said that the capsule left within a few minutes after you exited it. Is that correct?" asked Dr. Donovan looking first to Teresa and then Sonja.

Sonja answered. "Yes. At first we were afraid of the field and stayed away. It had attracted a number of very large Apatasaurs. They seemed to be curious. The sound of the harmonics seemed to attract them."

Again the two fathers exchanged looks. They were both wondering how these young children could grasp such a deep concept as harmonics. Teresa jumped into the conversation. "It was a few days before we were forced to jump back into the distortion field as the wall of fire from the comet approached."

"Comet? You didn't say anything about a comet before," said Sonja's mom.

Sonja said, "I thought I said we left because the comet was coming. Maybe I forgot to say that. Kyle said it might be the comet that wiped out the dinosaurs. He dragged Teresa and me back to the capsule and practically shoved us into the distortion field. The fire hit at the same time. I thought we were going to die! Kyle saved our lives."

Teresa added, "The sound of the violins filled the air and the capsule protected us from being killed. We could see the fire, but we couldn't feel it. The next thing I knew, we were back in the lab. I grabbed my shoestring out of the gel and put it back on. Then we got out in a hurry. That's when the capsule came back on. The sound of the violins...hundreds of them...in perfect harmony, as Kyle liked to say, came back and the capsule disappeared. When we all looked at our clothes, Kyle realized what had happened and chased us out of the lab and back into the lounge."

Dr. Donavan got up and began pacing. Dr. Bashan put his arm around his wife and Teresa and Sonja each put an arm around Teresa's mother who began to cry. She turned to her husband with pleading eyes and begged him, "Please, David, please bring our boy home!"

Dr. Donavan felt helpless and hopeless. Teresa and Sonja, however, knew that if anyone could figure out how to get out of this it would be Kyle. Teresa whispered to Sonja, "If I know Kyle, he'll bring the capsule back before he left and we'll never remember any of this. He won't even get grounded!"

CHAPTER TWENTY-TWO

The enormous animal beat its wings with slow methodical movements. They were over twenty feet wide—as big as a jetliner. Its keen eyesight scanned the ground for any unusual movement that might indicate an injured animal. The slow or jerky movements would stimulate the flying reptile's responses and, without thinking, it would begin a low, sweeping speed run at the prey in much the same way a jet fighter might try and fly below the radar as it stealthily engaged an enemy on the ground.

An odd movement below caused the creature to turn its head and focus on the activity. Something was moving, but it didn't immediately register as an injured animal. It was something about the *way* the animal moved that attracted its attention. It fanned out its broad wings and decelerated—first widening out the flight pattern. Then it quietly began pumping against the water-laden air thick with humidity that gave the creature the ability to fly in the first place.

Without taking its eye off the animal, it picked up speed as it cruised just above the treetops. There was no warning cry. Quietly, with only the swishing sound of its mighty wings thrusting it forward, it opened its mouth. The beak was long and full of jagged teeth—its jaws powerful. It would grab its prey and carry it off to its waiting young who would then rip the flesh from the animal. Sometimes while it was still alive.

***

Kyle ran from the pond as fast as his legs would carry him. There was something about the pair of eyes that frightened him to the bone. All attempts at reasoning, at the moment, were lost in his body's natural instincts: and they were telling him to flee from the potential predator. He didn't want to wait and find out what it was. The eyes were evil looking, almost demonic.

He spotted a large tree not far from the distortion field with an enormous root system at its base. He decided to head for it and changed direction. As he did, something hit him from behind and sent him sprawling to the ground. Fortunately, the grass was soft. Kyle turned to see what it was and his mouth opened wide—*a pterosaur*!

The creature thrust out its wings and began a tight turn. It screeched loudly and angrily, having lost the advantage of surprise. Now it would have to beat its wings with a great surge of power and chase its prey down.

Kyle jumped to his feet and began running toward the tree. It was a good twenty yards away. Instead of heading straight for the tree, however, he began changing direction rapidly. First he ran one way and then pivoted in the opposite direction as if he were dodging a competitor while dribbling a basketball down the court. It had the effect of confusing the pterosaur. It lunged at Kyle and snapped its mouth with a thud and clacking of its long teeth.

Kyle ran right past the tree he was running toward and grabbed a branch hanging low toward one side. It catapulted him around the trunk. As the creature tried to adjust, it caught one of its wings on the tree. Spinning wildly out of control it slammed head first into a palm tree and lay in a heap on the ground.

Kyle let go of the branch and ran back around the tree and jumped into a large space between the roots. It was partially hollowed out. It looked like an animal had been nibbling on it but left off in the middle. There were fresh wood chips all over the ground. He caught his breath and listened. Cautiously, he stuck his head out of the hollow and peered around the corner to see where the creature had gone. As he did, a beak full of jagged, sharp teeth lunged at his head and the pterosaur screeched.

***

Dr. Bashan and Dr. Donavan sat at the computer screen and analyzed the data stream. It was late that evening when they finally decided on a plan of action.

"We sent the capsule back approximately five years earlier according to the analysis I ran. It could be off by no more than 2%. Of course, there are variables that I can't factor in," said Dr. Bashan.

"So, if we believe the girls, the capsule would stay in transit until Kyle stepped back into the field. It won't go anywhere until that happens. But…what if one of us goes back, too? Wouldn't the capsule complete the transit?"

"Not necessarily. If one of us went back, we'd more than likely remain in transit as well. I don't know what effect that would have. We don't even know what is happening to the matter! All we know is that we vibrate the strings with the harmonics and the capsule appears in the past. Beyond that, we have a lot to learn. This is most unfortunate."

Dr. Donavan fought back the urge to panic. He always relied on his mental abilities, not his emotions, and he wasn't about to let that change now with so much at stake. "Perhaps…but maybe not. We have learned an enormous amount just from what the girls told us. What I find most peculiar is why Kyle would think that the string had anything to do with the capsule returning? How could he possibly know what that meant? I don't even know if it means anything!"

"But it is a variable. We shouldn't move the string."

"Ha! We can't move the string. It's like it isn't even there!"

"Yes," said Dr. Bashan thoughtfully. "It is like it isn't even there! Maybe that is the key! Somehow, the shoestring is in transit—in flux—not really matter and not quite energy. What if…what if the shoestring is causing the harmonics to vibrate just enough to pull it back in time to restore itself to completeness?"

Dr. Donavan had a puzzled look on his face. "Whoa, now you're losing me. What are you saying?"

"There is another theory that says something about all things in the material universe have a memory of other things they come in contact with. I don't remember all the specifics, but it's what popped into my head when I tried to understand the significance of the shoestring. I'm sure it has to do with string theory in some way—maybe it has to do with the different bits of matter vibrating at different frequencies. It's all connected somehow. We're just missing the pieces of the puzzle to solve it."

"If what you're saying is true, Kyle figured it out? I find that hard to believe."

"Where is your son?"

Dr. Donavan just stared. The point had been made. Kyle was doing things that were either entirely by accident, or he was brighter than he thought possible. Much brighter.

***

The pterosaur's breath was wretched. Kyle thrust himself into the tree hollow as far as he could. The beast was dragging one wing behind, but it didn't seem to stop it from trying to get at Kyle. It was very narrow-minded. Despite whatever pain it may or may not have been in at the moment, it still wanted to eat Kyle.

The jaw came around the corner and snapped at Kyle's leg. He kicked out and caught the creature in the snout. It drew blood and the monster screeched. Blood was also oozing down its forehead from the collision with the tree. It seemed oblivious to the pain and continued to snap at the tree opening.

Out of nowhere, a massive head appeared and huge powerful jaws with an enormous bird-like beak snapped down over the pterosaur's head. Kyle jumped and ran around behind the tree. A gigantic dinosaur with three horns on its head shook the pterosaur like a little broken toy. It dropped it to the ground, stepped on its body and began ripping flesh off in chunks and chewing the winged monster piece by piece.

A *Triceratops*!

The triceratops didn't appear to notice Kyle. It was satisfied with its prey. Kyle was getting desperate to leave this time period. It was clearly an "eat or be eaten" society and Kyle didn't think the odds were in his favor. As he watched, partly horrified and partly fascinated with the scene before him, something brushed against his leg. He jumped and yelled, "Ahhhh!"

When he turned to see what it was, there was nothing there. His leg felt wet—like a sponge had brushed against it. Out of the corner of his eye he saw something dart around a tree. It was a flash of gray.

He turned to check on the triceratops. It had consumed the pterosaur and was now heading back into the valley below. Satisfied he wasn't in any immediate danger, Kyle tiptoed toward the tree where he last saw movement. He heard a rustling coming from behind the tree and tried to peer around it. There was nothing there. He knew he didn't imagine it.

Coming all the way around the tree again, however, he found absolutely nothing. Puzzled, he scratched his head as he leaned casually against the tree. It had been a rough return so far and he was exhausted from all of the surprises. Now he even wished his sister was with him.

What am I saying? Have I gone completely insane?

He glanced back toward the distortion field. It was still shimmering and that gave him a sense of hope. *Maybe they have to launch it from the future again before I can get back inside?*

Deep in thought, he forgot about whatever had brushed against his leg—until something touched him again. "Ahhhh!" he screamed and jumped back. But again there was nothing there.

"Who…who's there? What are you? Come out so I can see whatever you are!"

Kyle peeked back around the tree and got the shock of his life.

"Priti!"

CHAPTER TWENTY-THREE

The sound of a hundred violins in perfect harmony filled the lab as the two doctors, their wives, Teresa and Sonja watched through the thick window of the vault door. The tubes and lines running through the ceiling and down to various computers glowed brilliant green and cast strange shadows across the anxious faces. Louder and louder the music grew and penetrated the earplugs each of them wore—except for Dr. Donavan.

They watched as the spinning swirling gel glowed with all of the colors of the rainbow as it pulsed up and down. Then it turned blue and then clear like water before shimmering out of existence.

Dr. Donavan was struck for the first time with the exhilarating feeling the music left him with. Never had he or Dr. Bashan allowed themselves to listen before. It was a hunch. Only he dared take the risk the harmonics wouldn't burst his eardrums. The girls had said Kyle insisted they hold their ears and close their eyes. But they didn't think that Kyle did. On a hunch, Dr. Donavan wanted to know if it affected Kyle's thinking.

He couldn't remember any time in his life that his mind felt so clear. So wonderful! What had the harmonics done to his mind, he wondered. Could the harmonics, responsible for the time capsule to move back in time, have caused changes in his brain chemistry somehow? Is that why Kyle was able to understand so much about it?

They all looked at the shimmering distortion field for several minutes, each in his or her own thoughts. There was a feeling of sadness among them—sadness and emptiness—and a feeling that Kyle might be gone forever.

Sonja looked down and pointed to something near the bottom of the distortion field. There, half visible and half invisible was Kyle's shoestring. Dr. Donavan felt the odd sensation of feeling confident. It wasn't like him to allow his feelings to dominate, yet, there it was. He was sure Kyle would be coming back. He knew it had something to do with the shoestring, but the answer eluded him. It lingered deep in the recesses of his mind. The answer was there—just beyond his grasp.

***

How far back have I gone? Could this really be Priti? She...I can't believe I'm calling it a she...doesn't act like she recognizes me. Of course she wouldn't! It has to be earlier in time or the planet would be a charred ruin and all of these creatures would be dead. Maybe it's only been a few years. Maybe Priti really is an adult animal. I thought so! Look at Toby. He's ten and he still acts like a puppy. Maybe this is just normal behavior for this species of dinosaur.

Kyle reached out as he had before and tried to make contact. "Come here, Priti. Come on," he cooed in his best Teresa imitation. The little raptor, not much bigger than his dog, cocked her head to one side and blinked.

"Here ya go, little lady. Here...try this," said Kyle as he peeled a piece of bark from the tree. He remembered Teresa and Sonja doing that. Then, ever so slowly, he sat down and crossed his legs to appear less frightening. Priti sniffed at the bark and then reached up and sniffed at Kyle's hand. She opened her mouth and Kyle saw the rows of sharp teeth. She hadn't hurt

106

him before, so he was sure she wouldn't bite if he didn't scare her.

Priti stuck out a long, thin, black tongue and touched Kyle's hand. She jerked back. Kyle didn't move an inch. Slowly, Priti reached out again and opened her mouth and gently took the bark in her teeth and withdrew it from Kyle's hand.

"That's a girl," he squeaked still trying to sound like his sister. "I don't believe I'm talking like this. And don't you tell Teresa when we get back! Okay?"

Priti was making gurgling sounds and nibbling at the bark that she had dropped to the ground. She seemed to be content at the moment. Kyle immediately started thinking of how he was going to get Priti back into the capsule. He hoped they had launched. If not…

Suddenly, Priti's head jerked back up. Her eyes were wide open. "What? What's wrong?"

Priti squealed and then hissed just before she bolted. Kyle remembered that behavior from before—always when there was danger. He turned around and, not twenty feet away stood a lone velociraptor bobbing its head and body up and down as it watched him with a cold hard look in its eyes.

***

"Paul," said Dr. Donavan sternly. "If Kyle manages to bring back a dinosaur, he could cause a *paradox*."

"David, that's just a sci-fi, Star-Trek concept. You've been watching too much television."

Dr. Donavan looked insulted. "I never watch television! A paradox is real, Paul. If Kyle brings back a dinosaur, it will throw the internal harmony of the entire universe off. The key to string theory has to do with the harmonics. Disharmony—which will be caused by bringing matter back out of time—could result in the destruction of the universe!" Dr. Donavan was almost yelling now. Dr. Bashan had never seen his partner so upset about anything before and it frightened him.

"You must be wrong, David! You have to be wrong. Because if you're right...this will have been our fault!"

Dr. Donavan now knew what he had to do. He loved his son dearly, but the fate of the universe was at stake.

I have to find a way of removing the shoestring. Even if it means I'll never see my son again.

CHAPTER TWENTY-FOUR

Kyle backed behind the tree while maintaining eye contact with the raptor. From just beyond the hill, he saw two more approaching rapidly. They were running like chickens—literally. Then several others appeared behind them. They all came up next to the first raptor. It hissed at the others and they engaged in striking and biting. David felt like they were arguing about who was going to eat him first.

He looked around to see if there was any way to hide. While they ran awkwardly, they appeared to be fast—too fast for him to outrun. The nearest other tree was a good twenty-five yards away. It didn't look to offer any more protection than where he was now. Priti had run down the hill toward the valley—*down the hill.* Perhaps he could outrun them. Every dinosaur he had observed since he had been here, both before and now, ran away from danger by running downhill!

With his options so narrow, he knew it was his only chance. Like a horse out of the starting gate—like a sprinter off the chocks—like a jet that had just hit its afterburner, Kyle ran as fast as he could. The raptors were caught off guard because of fighting amongst themselves. Kyle had a good head start before the raptors gave chase. It was then he realized his idea had been wrong. The raptors lifted their arms and feather-like appendages, which lifted them slightly off the ground and increased their speed.

Kyle passed the area where the pterosaur had first tried to get him. He was almost on even ground now and the raptors were close—so close he could hear them hissing at him. Occasionally, one of the raptors would nudge the other in an attempt to gain an advantage. It would slow them all down just enough for Kyle to increase the distance—but it wouldn't last long.

Up ahead he could see the pond where he had washed his clothes. A thought about what might be at the bottom frightened him, but the real fear of being torn to shreds by the velociraptors was the more immediate threat. Kyle headed straight for the pond. As he reached the pond's edge, there was no time to stop and consider his actions. One of the raptors had caught up and grabbed his shirt. With a valiant leap, Kyle tore free from the raptor and dove headfirst into the water.

The raptor stopped and the others caught up and fought voraciously over Kyle's shirt ripping it to shreds. Kyle came to the surface and treaded water as quietly as he could. He had no idea whether the raptors could swim or not, but they appeared to think they had their prey.

One by one they left off—still hungry—and went looking for a more satisfying meal. Kyle decided the best course of action was to swim across the pond, which was only about as wide as an Olympic sized swimming pool. As he turned, the water began to boil in front of him. It was then he remembered the evil-looking eyes that had stared back from beneath the surface of the water. With all his heart, Kyle wanted to be home. He wished he had never set foot in the capsule in the first place; wished he had never even heard of string theory.

Something broke through the surface of the water directly in front of him. An enormous head with yellow eyes emerged and stared back with a look of surprise on its face.

***

Again the old saying of his mother came to mind: "Out of the frying pan and into the fire." Only this time it was out of the fire and into the inferno, he thought. Hopelessly trapped, he waited for the creature to snap his head off or swallow him whole or whatever it was going to do. Kyle closed his eyes and waited, and waited, but nothing happened. Slowly he opened his eyes.

The water monster was still there, but next to it were several smaller heads. *Oh great, it appears the whole family is eating out and I'm the main course!*

One of the smaller animals began to move cautiously around Kyle. Two others moved in the opposite direction. The larger monster stayed perfectly still. Kyle thought it resembled a dolphin, but there wasn't any blowhole. It had slits down each side of its neck. It did have a perpetual smile on its face, but Kyle wasn't about to believe that it was all that happy to see him. Again, as with the raptors, he decided to try an offensive move. However, instead of being aggressive, he swam toward one of the smaller animals and reached his hand out to touch it. It disappeared below the surface.

When Kyle looked around to see what happened to the others, he noticed that they too were gone. The larger monster moved toward Kyle and nudged him. Its head was the size of a Volkswagen beetle. Kyle reached out and gently stroked its head. The monster nudged Kyle again. It was only then that Kyle realized its mouth was very tiny. He doubted he could even get his fist in it. It reminded Kyle of the mouth of a seahorse—long but tiny compared to its body.

The smaller creatures returned and it was the same with them—small mouths. They appeared to be bolder with Kyle near the larger one and swam over to him. Gently he reached out and touched one on the nose. It stayed. The others all got in the act and began to nuzzle Kyle. He pet them all including the larger one. After a few minutes, Kyle decided enough was enough and headed for the shore. The larger one, which Kyle assumed was the mother, blocked his way. Now he became concerned. Although they weren't aggressive, he was in danger of becoming exhausted. He really didn't expect the animals would be able to comprehend his inability to submerge as they could.

A high-pitched whistle came out of the mouth of the mother. Its eyes, softer than when it first approached, had now become cold and hard again. While these creatures didn't have any teeth, it was clear to Kyle they could easily drag him below the surface and drown him. Kyle shoved the mother aside with as much force as he could muster. She didn't budge.

It whistled loudly again and the babies disappeared below the surface. As to exactly what was going on, Kyle was clueless. Now it was only the mother and he. She whistled angrily at Kyle and the sound hurt his ears. *Disharmony.* Something was wrong. Loud noises meant that something was not in tune with the material universe. If he didn't get to shore soon, *he* was going to be in disharmony with the universe.

Then he heard it. A hiss came from behind the large docile animal. On the opposite shore, the raptors had gathered and were waiting for the rest of their dinner. The shirt had served as only a poor appetizer. Was the creature actually trying to protect him, he wondered? Perhaps it had adopted him and was trying to convince him to dive. The animal didn't know that wasn't an option open to Kyle, but she seemed intent on protecting him.

She whistled again, more loudly this time and nudged him. Even if he wanted to dive below the surface, he couldn't. He was just too tired and out of breath. The creature shook its head and dove below the surface. Now Kyle was alone. He couldn't swim across the pond anymore since the raptors were there. If he emerged from where he had entered the first time, it was a simple matter for them to run around the pond and chase him down.

He looked in the direction of the raptors and tried to come up with a solution. Then without warning, an enormous beast the size of a school bus came flying out of the water and landed on several of the raptors. Two of them escaped and went screaming in the opposite direction. Kyle hadn't realized just how large the creature was. He decided to head back across the pond before the docile monster decided to take him home to be a part of the family.

He crawled out onto the shore and heard a gentle whistle behind him. The mother's head was resting on the shore—her eyes soft pools of gold and yellow once again. Kyle reached over and patted the enormous head.

"Thanks, girl. Sorry I can't join you...although part of me wishes I could. I wouldn't mind having you around to protect me."

Three little heads popped up again behind their mother. All of them were whistling—in perfect harmony.

***

The unusual creatures went back to the depths of the pond. Kyle wondered just how deep it must be to house such huge creatures. As he thought about it, he heard the cracking sound of a branch from behind him. Nearly ready to leap back into the water, he began laughing at the creature that was bopping up and down and bending low to the ground and hissing. It was almost as if Priti were pretending to be a velociraptor.

Kyle sat down and Priti came over and put her head in his lap. He scratched the rough, leather-like feathers and Priti cooed and purred a deep gurgling sound.

"Come on, Priti. We have to get to the capsule. You and I are heading back to the future, baby!"

***

Dr. Donavan didn't say anything to anyone—not even his partner—about what he was about to do. He was sure someone would try and stop him. He knew they wouldn't understand and he didn't have time to explain.

It had taken him all night to work out the disruptor and key in the opposite frequency for every set of harmonics in the computer. It had taken virtually all of the remaining space on the banks of hard drives in the system to come up with the data. Once he disrupted the field, the shoestring would materialize and he would have to remove it. The capsule would complete its journey, but Kyle would never be able to return to the same time period ever again. He would be lost and have to live the rest of his life in the past.

Dr. Donavan stood before the door to the vault with the disruptor in his hand. It was the size of a small transistor radio. The sound was concentrated to shoot straight out of the laser beam he had attached to the front of the device. The concentrated beam of discordant sounds—a match for every harmony the capsule created—would be dissolved. The string would return along with the capsule.

There was always the possibility of going back in time after that and rescuing Kyle—if they could pinpoint the exact moment. It was the only hope he had. But if he was too late…

Dr. Donavan felt himself give way to tears. Large ones pooled under his eyes and fell to the floor. He only hoped his wife would forgive him for what he was about to do.

The vault door opened and Dr. Donavan went in. He placed the disruptor as close to the string as possible and set the timer. Then he left. In thirty seconds, Kyle was going to be stranded in the past some 65 million years ago.

CHAPTER TWENTY-FIVE

Priti followed Kyle as he headed back to the distortion field. She occasionally ran up and grabbed his pant leg and pulled. Kyle had already lost his shirt.

"Knock it off, doof-a-saurus! You want me to call you that instead of Priti? Huh? Do ya?"

He looked around. There weren't any other dinosaurs in sight. "Come on, Priti. Wanna see Teresa and Sonja?" Priti cocked her head as if trying to understand him. "You can't remember them. But you will. No doubt you'll be treated real nice. They're going to be surprised to see you!"

Not twenty yards from the distortion field, it appeared their good fortune had come to an end. The two raptors that had escaped were standing next to the distortion field and it looked like they were hungrier than ever.

***

Dr. Donavan watched through the window as the timer ticked down. It was at 15 seconds. He closed his eyes and fought back the urge to panic. He felt he was killing his own son—sacrificing him to save the universe.

He peeked as the timer passed 2 seconds.

***

Kyle froze. Priti froze as well. Everything appeared to be moving in slow motion. Not just from the situation, he noticed, but literally in slow motion. One of the raptors was in the process of opening its mouth to scream at Kyle, but no sound was coming out.

Then he heard music. Not the perfect harmony of the violins, but a low, frightening cello sound and it was coming from the distortion field!

Kyle seized the opportunity and scooped up Priti in his arms. She felt like she weighed a hundred pounds. Priti didn't even react. She could have been a robot or a giant stuffed toy filled with rocks.

Kyle ran toward the distortion field where he could see the slightest shimmering of greenish blue appearing. It was spinning ever so slowly. One of the raptors moved its head and began to open its mouth, but Kyle was moving in real time while, for reasons he couldn't understand, everything else was moving much slower.

Kyle dove into the distortion field with Priti in his arms and squeezed. Then he blacked out.

***

When he came to, Priti was licking his face with her disgustingly long, black and very wet tongue. Had he made it? He jumped up, sending Priti sprawling.

I'm in the capsule! Are we back in the future?

He looked through the green gel. It was dark outside. *Maybe there's no one in the lab?*

Then he saw a light. A single focused point of light shone into the capsule and on him — then on Priti. Priti moved closer to Kyle.

"Well, come on, Priti. Let's see who's in the welcoming committee. Boy, are they going to be surprised to see you!"

Kyle felt around for the opening. The gel parted and he stepped out. He looked up and was surprised to see a full moon shining down on him. Several black clouds passed in front and cast shadows across the ground. It illuminated trees and bushes. He wasn't in the lab!

A figure approached and shone a light in his face. "Kyle? Is it really you? And Priti? My god!"

Kyle looked at the figure in front of him as the light from the moon illuminated her face. He recognized her!

"Mom? Is that really you?"

The older woman with gray hair reached out and hugged him tightly. Priti simply bobbed up and down nearby and cocked her head to one side.

"Mom, where am I? What happened to the lab? Why are you so...*old*?" he said looking at her.

"Kyle. I'm not Mom. It's me...Teresa.

THE END